LEYA

Sphere of Vision  Book One

BONNIE FERRANTE

ISBN   978-1-928064-17-6

First edition title Desiccate

Thank you to Writers Northwest for all their help editing this novel especially Sharon Irvine and Tessa Soderburg for reading the whole thing.

Thank you to Pauline O'Neill and Jamie Maltman for proofreading my final copy.

Thank you to my husband, Fred, for all his help in countless ways.

A huge thank you to the Ontario Arts Council for their generous Writers Works in Progress Grant.

ONTARIO ARTS COUNCIL
CONSEIL DES ARTS DE L'ONTARIO

50 YEARS OF ONTARIO GOVERNMENT SUPPORT OF THE ARTS
50 ANS DE SOUTIEN DU GOUVERNEMENT DE L'ONTARIO AUX ARTS

3

I

Although the villagers rose with the sun to work the fields, attend to the animals, bake their bread, and begin their long list of chores, for me, Leya Truelong, this was a day like no other. Today, Wren River was touched by the fantastic.

As smoke from the brick ovens rose in thin columns over the thatched and wood shingle roofs, I left the village and headed down a path toward a clearing in the woods. Perhaps, this year, for the first time in my parents' memory, a fourteen-year-old from our village would be chosen. Perhaps it would be me.

I looked down at my soft, brown, suede boots, ankle high, with wrap around fronts that tied on the sides. They were stained and worn. I wished I had something prettier to wear, but at least these were solid and in reasonable shape, unlike my dress, which was held together by a whisper and a prayer. Ma had lent me a lace collar to hide the frayed neckline. Perhaps my boots would count in my favor. The Mistress of the Sphere of Vision might recognize that I was not a frivolous, pampered girl. Not like the tanner's daughter, in her glistening leather shoes. Not like the silversmith's daughter, whose canvas shoes sparkled with silver buttons. Not like the mayor's daughter, Jenifair, in red satin slippers lined with felt. My boots were those of a hard-working, serious young lady, one who had to labor for everything she owned.

Every spring a Master, and every summer a Mistress, each from their own Sphere of Vision, came to the village to examine any fourteen-year-olds. They rode in on their great horses, wearing majestic robes that cost more than we could save in a year. Sometimes there was no one of the right age, so they rode on without pause, or they avoided the village altogether. This year there were four girls to be judged.

I saw the first three return rejected. The tanner's daughter seemed angry. The silversmith's daughter seemed bored. Jenifair, who already had everything a girl could want, seemed embarrassed. I was waiting on the doorstep for her return. Unexpectedly, she said, "Good morning," as she passed our little cottage. I was so shocked; I didn't think to respond until she had gone. Usually she looked through me as though I was made of glass.

I guess she was hedging her bets, just in case I was accepted since she wasn't. At least, I didn't think she was. Wouldn't she be excited? But, this was just one of many opportunities for Jenifair. Her future was already bright. For me, this was the one and only chance to break free of a life of drudgery and fear. One possibility for happiness or heartbreak, and it all depended on my eyes.

Since the announcement of our upcoming examination, I had expected the village girls, led by Jenifair, to continue mocking me for my clothes, shoes, rough and red hands, and crooked teeth. Instead, they hadn't said a word. I realized they had no more control over the outcome today than I did. Their wealth, education, and social standing were worthless when evaluated by a Mistress. For one marvelous moment, I was their equal.

A mourning dove called, its plaintive notes breaking the silence. "Don't run, don't run," it warned.

I wanted to run. I wanted to fly. To be there. To have it done. To know. To know now.

I fought the urge to race down the dirt path. It was foolish to hope, but I could no more crush hope than I could turn inside out.

I had not had a chance to see the lucky two girls travelling with Mistress Sangra. They had been chosen from previous villages. Maybe they were ordinary peasant girls like me, with dreams and hopes and theirs were coming true.

My youngest brother, Albair, told me those two chosen girls were refilling water bags and buying food supplies in Wren River while the Mistress examined prospective Novices.

"I heard the Mistress spoke Granjese," said Albair. "She's light-skinned and stocky. I think she may have originally come from our region."

A Granja Mistress. She would understand our struggles. Being one of us, perhaps she would be more inclined to overlook my faults. But, I wouldn't speak Granjese to her. Ma insisted we speak Esfera, the cross-region language developed by the Spheres. I could speak Granjese; I wouldn't be able to survive in Wren River without it. But at home, we spoke Esfera, the language of the educated. I had never heard anyone from outside our region speak it. I hoped my accent wasn't terrible. Would she admire my effort or think I was putting on airs?

I was the last scheduled for the Mistress to consider. I examined my surroundings, suddenly aware that this might be my last summer in Wren River for a while. The morning sun illuminated purple clusters of mock vervain and sunny coneflower that lined the winding trail. I felt as though the radiant flowers were wishing me good luck. Wealth, fame, power, could be waiting for me at the end of the trail. No more thrice patched clothes. No more rationing coal. No more eating the wormy vegetables and selling the best.

Without intention, my feet moved faster and faster toward the clearing where Mistress Sangra waited. "Think before you speak or act," was Ma's advice. "Consider all the consequences of your choices. I know what it's like to be young and I don't want you making the same mistakes I did." Advice I heard often, for good reason. She never did confess what her mistakes were though.

I realized I was rushing. It would be a poor first impression to arrive out of breath and windblown. I forced myself to slow. Be calm, be calm. I took deep breaths. I smoothed back my hair. When had this trail become so long?

This opportunity would never come again. I was terrified of being chosen and all that would mean, but, being rebuffed would be even more unbearable. I was the third child of five in my family to be examined. When Thomis turned fourteen, and later Maark, neither had been selected by the Masters to attend their Sphere of Vision. Ma hadn't said a negative word, but I saw the hopeful look extinguished in her eyes when neither of them was chosen.

On the other hand, the Masters had a reputation for harshness. Some Pesca and Miniria parents refused to let their sons be examined. Understandable, considering the wealth of those regions. I had never heard of a Granja turning down the opportunity though. We forest and farm people could never match a graduate of a Sphere for wealth or power. Even our mayor did not come close. Still, I was secretly relieved that neither Thomis nor Maark were chosen. Rumor said males were not the same after their time with the Masters. I did not want to see my brothers broken.

Even though the Mistresses were reputed to be kinder, it was not an easy thing to leave one's family. This morning, I had avoided looking at my mother's face. I had gone about my chores as though it was an ordinary day, until the appointed time. The Mistress had arrived in Wren River last night and stayed, with the two selected girls, in the best inn. She hired a local woman to set up morning examinations with all the fourteen-year-old girls. I barely slept last night considering what might happen.

In the clearing, the Mistress stood with her hands tucked in the opposite sleeves of her long red robe. I felt the woman's eyes studying my every step. I took another deep breath, trying to calm my pounding heart and forced a shaky smile to my lips.

"Step into the circle, Leya Truelong," said the Mistress in Granjese when I approached. Her voice was strong. She was but a snippet taller than me. She wore her long, flaming brown threaded with grey pinned up in complicated braids. Intricate, fine leather sandals with silver studs graced her feet.

I noted the circle carved into the sandy earth, and stepped inside. The Mistress stepped in to face me.

I replied in Esfera, "What should I—"

"Sha," ordered the Mistress.

I clamped my mouth shut. A light wind rustled the leaves on the trees and passed through my thin green dress. Mistress Sangra placed her hands on my shoulders and, with wide unblinking eyes, stared into my face. My heartbeat surged in my ears.

Bright red eyes, like a ripe tomato, studied me. I suppressed a nervous giggle at the thought. Some Visions were worth more than others. I'd heard of a woman who had the ability to control cloud formations. The best she could offer was a little shade. Surely, a Mistress should have a powerful, important Vision. What was the point otherwise?

The Mistress leaned in closer. When her red eyes burrowed into me, mine stung to the point of tears. It felt as though something tunneled through each iris and into my brain, like a peppery worm. Her fingers dug into my shoulders. No one told me it would hurt so much.

II

I refused to cry, but my whole body trembled. I was grateful only one village girl at a time was sent for examination. How humiliating it would be to break down in front of the others.

I told myself to just breathe calmly. It would be over soon. Courage was probably part of the test. I wished the Mistress would hurry. The stinging in my eyes changed to swelling, as though they would burst like dropped eggs. I couldn't squirm. I couldn't ask questions. I gritted my teeth. Standing still took all my control.

The Mistress's red eyes narrowed as she scanned my face. She leaned in close enough for her rosemary scented breath to waft on my cheek. I fought the urge to step back; it was unnerving having a stranger so close. What would happen if I left the circle?

She smiled, dropped her hands, and pulled back, blinking. The pain faded.

"And what kind of girl are you?" asked the Mistress, now speaking Esfera.

"A good girl, I hope," I said, dipping my small frame in deference. I pushed a wayward strand of hair behind my ear.

"You hope?" said the Mistress with a touch of humor in her voice.

I opened my mouth, shut it, and then gave an awkward shrug.

"Just good, not special?" asked Mistress Sangra.

Was that a trick question? Did she want me to be modest or did the Mistress want to know if I had discovered any unusual talent? I wiped my sweating hands on my threadbare dress. "No, Mistress. I'm not special. Just a little odd."

The Mistress grinned and pointed to my left eye and then my right one. Her nails were well-manicured and her hands were smooth. "Because of these?"

"Yes, Mistress - one blue and one green," I said. "The only other creature in town with two different colored eyes is Jumble . . . uh, the blacksmith's tomcat. He—" I pushed down the urge to tell more about the animal and its thievery. Jenifair called me Jumblina and said I was a ratter. She said I would be lucky if the cat would have me for a mate while the other girls made meowing sounds.

Mistress Sangra laughed. "You are luckier than the blacksmith's cat, child. Yours are not ordinary eyes. I sense Vision potential in you, possibly double potential."

"Oh, my!" I crossed my hands over my thin body. A thrill shot through me. I had a chance, I had a chance. I swallowed, trying not to look impatient.

"Double potential is unusual, but not unheard of," said Mistress Sangra. "Do not get too excited. Seldom are both fulfilled. It is a knife that cuts both ways. Are you an ambitious girl?" The Mistress clamped her hand on my right upper arm.

I hoped I wasn't trembling on the outside as much as I was on the inside. The size of my ambition could fill the universe, but I knew that answer would not be well received.

"I would appreciate a chance at a better life. I'm not afraid of hard work and I always try my best."

I tried not to sound defensive. No one had ever asked me such personal questions before. I felt terribly exposed, but was afraid to hold anything back. Was it wise to deceive a Mistress?

Who knew what Vision power this Mistress possessed? Perhaps she could see into my heart.

Mistress Sangra dropped her hand, leaned back a little, tilted her head, and studied me intently.

"That is an excellent answer. Ours is a difficult path. I suspect you are used to hard work. You seem neither lazy nor pampered. I know, from personal experience, that the life of a Granja is usually a struggle for the basics. The rewards are great for a Mistress of the Sphere, but they do not come easily."

I glanced at the Mistress's silken, red robe edged with silver and her pure white gown beneath. A silver clasp with the Sphere's insignia was pinned to the elaborately embroidered collar.

What would it feel like to touch cloth like that? To wear it every day? How many robes did she own? Who did the embroidery? I would be happy if my family had clothing that was not covered in patches. Happy if we had waterproof coats for rainy days. Happy if our shoes were sturdy, and our boots didn't leak.

I scolded myself. I needed to pay attention to what the Mistress was saying. Was ambition good or bad? I knew fewer Novices were being accepted yearly. I didn't know why.

"What do you want?" asked Mistress Sangra.

I stammered, "P-pardon?"

"What would you hope to gain by becoming a Novice of the Sphere of Vision?"

"Oh. I want to be a help to my Ma and Pa. To make things easier for them." And to never again be mocked by anyone.

The Mistress smiled. "And when you are a grown woman on your own?"

I bit my lip. "I want to be as good a person as my Ma, no matter where I go or what I do."

My amazing Ma, prematurely graying brown hair pinned up in a neat bun, tired eyes, but a smile on her face. Her life was hard, but she took simple joy in her family and in being of service to others. Always in control, always patient. I could never be like that when I was struggling, every day, to get by. If I had more wealth and power, then I would find it easier to give, to think of others.

Mistress Sangra nodded. "What makes your Ma a good person?"

I considered my stocky Ma, the anchor for our busy family. "Kindness, generosity, and forgiveness."

The Mistress crossed her arms and narrowed her eyes. "Has she had much to forgive?"

"She has five children, and we aren't perfect." I glanced nervously away and then whispered, "I make a lot of mistakes."

The Mistress tapped her fingertip on her lip, considering my answer. "Do you learn from your mistakes?"

"I hope so, Mistress. I try to." I didn't always succeed.

Mistress Sangra nodded. "Effort is the way to merit. You did not pull away when your eyes began to hurt. How much pain can you handle?"

I squirmed. "I don't know, Mistress. As much as I have to, I guess."

"There will be pain. Mastering your Vision comes at a price."

I said nothing.

"Would you like to be able to help more than your own family? Would you be willing to spend your life in the service of the Sphere above all else?"

I nodded eagerly. Sure, sure, whatever it took.

"You would be financially secure, but there would be times when you would be expected to provide your services for free to deserving people."

I nodded again. Who decided who was deserving? My family deserved better, but no one had ever helped them. My breathing sped up. "Yes, Mistress. I would be honored."

"Would you vow to put service to the Sphere before personal wealth or glory?" The Mistress's voice seemed to fill the clearing. The grasses and wildflowers, songbirds and squirrels, and even the wind seemed to pause to hear. "Would you be willing to work hard, face personal discomfort, even physical pain?"

My toes wiggled inside my boots. "Of course, Mistress."

"Then say, 'I vow to do so.'"

I repeated, "I vow to do so."

"You will not be allowed to return to Wren River for at least two years and not be allowed to leave the Sphere of Vision unless instructed to do so by a Mistress. You will focus entirely on your studies. Think well before you nod again. It is a commitment not to be taken lightly."

I paused for a second, and then nodded once more, my whole body bobbing. My mother would struggle without my help, but one day I would be able to repay her for the sacrifice.

Mistress Sangra laughed softly and then tapped me on the left shoulder, forehead, right shoulder, and heart.

"You are accepted to join the Mistresses' Circle of Vision."

I clamped my hands over my mouth to stop from screaming with excitement.

"Welcome, little sister," she said.

"Thank you," I responded, a little too loudly.

"From this moment on you will be known simply as Leya."

"Really? Why?" I blurted.

"Our girls do not use their last names at the Sphere. Everyone is equal. There are no social classes, no grudges or allegiances to be brought to the Sphere of Vision. No matter which of the four regions we were born into, we are all Vision Sisters now. I am pleased you can speak Esfera so well. It is the only language officially spoken at the Sphere." Mistress Sangra gestured widely. "If you are successful, you can then choose your own last name upon completion, to reflect your experience and skill."

"So Sangra isn't your first name?"

Mistress Sangra blinked. "No, we only use our first names in private."

"So I won't be called Leya Truelong when I'm finished the training?"

"You will always be Leya. But, this is not the time to be thinking about the end of your journey. This is a time for beginnings."

I nodded. "I understand." If I was allowed to choose, maybe I would be able to use my birth surname after I left. It felt strange to separate myself from my family, not daughter, not sister, a non-entity. But, I would have a new identity, one equal to, no above the daughters of tanners, silversmiths, and even mayors.

"From this moment on, whenever you greet a Mistress of Vision or a Vision Novice you are to say, "May you always see clearly. Repeat it."

"May you always see clearly."

"The response to that is, May your vision be pure. Repeat."

"May your vision be pure."

The Mistress stepped out of the circle. Her voice lowered into a conversational tone. "You will leave immediately with me. I will gather up the other two girls and stow their purchases before coming to get you. You are the only girl chosen from Wren River. The only girl in a long, long time. Take only as much time as needed to pack and say goodbye. You will receive new clothing at the Sphere of Vision, so you only need to bring sturdy clothes for travelling. Pack only what can be carried behind you on a horse."

I started. "I don't have a horse, Mistress."

Mistress Sangra smiled. "Do not worry. I brought one for you."

"How—"

"Mistress Prophet has the Vision of divination," said the Mistress dismissively. "She tells each Mistress how many horses will be needed. Now, quickly, go. Time is passing."

I turned and took three steps, stopped, turned back, and curtseyed. "Thank you, Mistress."

"You are welcome. Now hurry." She waved me away. "We will come for you."

I didn't even attempt to walk on the way back. I did not want to give the Mistress the chance to change her mind. My feet flew over the ground. While the idea of living with strangers made my stomach flutter, I yearned for a chance to see what lay beyond my tiny world. I would be prompt and obedient and eager. I would make my family proud. I would transform all our lives for the better.

III

I raced toward home; the small, wood-framed and plaster cottage with the thatched roof seemed suddenly precious. I burst inside letting the wooden door slam open against the inside wall. My parents and brothers were waiting in the main room; they jumped at the bang. For once, no one scolded me.

There had been a time when flinging open the door was a daily occurrence. No matter how many times my parents told me to watch what I was doing, I forgot in the excitement of the moment. It had taken hitting my little sister in the face and making her nose bleed to break me of the habit. I still felt a cringe of shame when I thought of it. Today, my mind was on other things.

Panting, my hand pressed against my chest, my hair tossed about my damp face, I announced, "I was chosen! Sweet Mother Earth, I was chosen! Can you believe it?"

Ma dropped the shirt she was sewing, and Pa tightly gripped the harness he was mending. At the other end of the long wooden table, Albair and Maark set down their knives and the potatoes they were peeling. Albair, my younger brother by a year, stared at me, his mouth falling open. For once he had nothing to say. Maark looked from one brother to the other, checking to be sure he had heard right. Thomis, the eldest, set down the peas he had been shelling and clapped his hands loudly together. Everyone stared at me as I stepped further into the room. Little Sarah was absent; Ma had sent her berry picking behind the house to get her out of our hair. Usually, there were not so many people helping in the kitchen, but everyone wanted to stay close, waiting for my return.

Ma gasped and covered her mouth. My brothers' eyes widened as they slapped and punched each other with excitement.

Pa put down the harness and smiled broadly enough to show his back teeth. He ran his hand through his thinning, brown hair, his eyes gleaming with pride. He walked over to Ma and squeezed her shoulder. They exchanged a private look. Then he whooped, strode over, and gave me a bear hug, picking me up, and twirling me around as though I was still a little girl.

"Pa, Pa, set me down," I said.

He did. We both stumbled a little, out of breath.

"I have only a little time to pack and say goodbye." I spoke quickly. "I was the last person to be examined so the Mistress is getting ready to leave now. She'll be coming for me soon. What should I do? She has a horse for me to ride. Do we have a bag I can use to carry my things?" My body twitched in different directions, and my eyes flittered around the room. "I suppose I could wrap things in a sheet. If I can have a sheet. Is it alright if I take one? I could send it back somehow after I get there." I tucked my hair behind my ears. "Mistress Sangra has given me a horse. Imagine that. While not given, really. At least a horse to ride, I mean—"

"Take a breath, Leya," said my father as he patted my shoulder. "Let's all just take a moment here. This kind of thing doesn't happen every day." He was much taller than I, or my Ma. His bare arms flexed with wiry muscles as he clasped my shoulders and drew me in for another hug.

"Oh, Pa," my lips trembled. "I have to leave you all! I won't see you again for two years!"

"What do you mean — *have to*?" asked Ma as she finished stowing the needle, folding the sewing, and tucking it into her wooden box. "Did you not have a choice?" She stood, placed her hands on her hips and studied my face. Pa dropped his hands from my shoulders as Ma stepped forward.

Ma's intense gaze was so similar to the Mistress's it was unnerving.

"Yes, I had a choice," I said. "She asked me questions to be sure I wanted this. She told me over and over that it was a huge commitment, and it wouldn't be easy. I do want to go. I really, really do. I want it more than anything."

I would do whatever it took to break free of the grueling work for little reward that lay ahead of me.

"Alright, then, if you are sure," said Ma. She tidied her hair and straightened her apron. "Come here, my angel."

She pulled me in for a tight hug. My brothers crowded around and alternately patted my back and joined the hug. I could tell they hadn't expected this.

"Ma, do you know how much wealth I could bring to our family?" I said as I untangled myself from the group. "Did you see the Mistress's robes and jewelry and the horses?"

My mother raised her eyebrows. "Wealth would be wonderful, but not at the cost of your happiness. Don't do this for us."

Ma's remark stunned me into silence. Why would I turn down the best chance I would ever have for success?

"Ma," I did a small dance. "I am happy. I'm very happy!"

My mother nodded, her eyes suddenly filling with tears. She turned to her oldest child. "Thomis, would you lend Leya your bag for her things?"

"Of course, Ma." His deep voice broke. He smiled at me and nodded twice. Thomis fancied himself my protector, scolding the other two boys when their teasing and roughhousing brought me to tears.

Ma glanced around our kitchen. "Do you need to bring food, Leya?"

"I don't know." I had raced off without asking anything. What did I need? What would be provided? How could I have been so brainless? Were the other girls only shopping for food for themselves? Did I have to provide my own? I chewed on my lip.

"I think not," said my father. "The Mistress will provide food, I'm sure. She would want the girls to have the same food and be well-fortified for their journey. Once a Novice is accepted, they are under the care and protection of the Mistresses or Masters."

"Of course. Still, the child might want a familiar snack," said Ma. "We don't know what kind of food the Mistress will provide. Too much strangeness all at once can be upsetting." She opened a cupboard, took down a white, linen bundle and set it on the wooden counter. "Maark, cut your sister some cheese and wrap it in this clean cloth." She picked up a small basket and passed it to my younger brother. "Albair get some of the hazelnuts she likes. It'll be a taste of home while she's travelling. Husband—"

"Now, you take a breath," said my father as he took Ma's hand. "We will take as long as we take. No use flopping about like beached fish."

Ma looked at Pa, smiled, and nodded, her eyes bright with unshed tears. He gave her small hand a squeeze. They looked into each other's eyes. Ma's lips trembled and Pa swallowed several times.

I pretended not to notice and went to my room to pack. The room smelled of wild roses that Sarah had stuck in a jar, their stems now bent and blossoms drooping. There was a big single bed, a row of pegs, and a chest of drawers, all made by my father. The boys had only boxes for their clothes. Pa had made the chest especially for his girls, carving the handles into rough leaves. It may not have been as expensive or elegant as some, but it was priceless to me. I collapsed on the bed, the full shock of what was happening finally sinking in.

IV

Stretched out on the bed, I looked around the room, wondering if things would be the same when I returned. The small window held heavy, brown curtains my mother had woven and stitched. Sarah had complained they were dull, but I was grateful for the thick, dark color keeping out the hot sun in summer. Our bedroom faced east and, although Ma always got up with the sun, on special days, she let us sleep in a little longer. What time did Novices rise at the Sphere of Visions?

I removed my green dress and slipped into brown work pants and a loose grey shirt. I took my brown woolen cloak down from the hook and placed it in the bottom of Thomis' travel bag. I folded my two dresses, other pants and shirt, and spare undergarments and added them to the bag.

My seven-year-old sister, Sarah, and I shared this tiny room. No doubt she would enjoy the extra space, but we would miss each other. How would it feel to fall asleep without my sister chattering about the day? Who would keep Sarah's feet warm at night?

I sat on the bed and put my hands over my face. I thought leaving would be easy. My whole life, I've wanted nothing more than to escape, but I wished I could bring my family with me, even annoying Albair who wanted everything I had and would probably complain the whole time. Maybe when his turn came, he would be picked as well. I took a deep breath, smoothed my clothes, and stood up.

Sarah's drawing of the family caught my attention. She was still in school, but I had had to leave to help with the farm. In the picture, everyone's head was much too big for their body, everyone's smile too big for their face. I was the only one whose smile was a single line since I didn't like to show my crooked teeth. I carefully folded the picture three times and placed it in my bag.

18

My hands clenched. What if I wasted two years of my life and never mastered my Vision, whatever that Vision was? I'd heard stories of girls returning home no different than when they had left, except for being older and bitterly disappointed. Well, as Pa said, you don't gain anything by not trying. I took one last look around, tidied Sarah's shabby rag doll on the pillow, straightened my shoulders and opened the door.

My family waited in the main room. My father's skill as an amateur carpenter was evident in the table, chairs, shelves, and counter. What would it be like to sit and eat and sleep on furniture made by strangers? Who would sit at the head of the table?

Ma quickly wiped her eyes on her apron. My family smiled thinly. Albair's eyebrows were squeezed together and he opened and closed his mouth several times. It was a rare day he couldn't think of something to say. Maybe he was downcast by my departure. Who would he torment in my place? Sarah was too only seven and my older brothers wouldn't tolerate him teasing such a little girl too much. Maark intently picked at a fingernail, avoiding my eyes.

The front door opened as Sarah returned. She was dressed in a knee-length, blue skirt and a white short-sleeved shirt. Her hair was pulled back into a ponytail, crooked, and coming undone, as usual. Her boney knees were dirty, and her lips were blue with berry stains. She carried a small covered basket. Her big eyes looked from one family member to another, frowning at their strange expressions and the large bag in my arms.

"Was— was she chosen?" she asked in a tiny voice.

Ma nodded as she took the bag from me. Sarah put the basket on the floor and ran into my arms. Albair walked over, picked up the basket, peeled back the cover and frowned at the small number of berries. He set the basket on the counter by the window.

"Don't look so distraught," I said as I stroked my sister's light, brown hair. "It'll be alright." I couldn't let Sarah know how scared I was.

I paused and picked a leaf out of a tangle of her hair. No matter how much Ma brushed it, Sarah's hair was always wild. Yet, my little sister refused to let anyone cut it. She wanted long hair like mine.

"I'll only be gone for about two years," I said, making my voice deliberately cheerful. "Keep busy, and I'll be back before you know it."

"Two years!" cried Sarah. "Why so long? Can't you come home for visits?"

"The Mistresses know best," said Ma. "It seems in the past some girls came home for holidays and got themselves into trouble before they knew how to properly control their Visions."

"Can I visit her there?" Sarah pleaded.

Ma shook her head. "Too far for us to go. You can write to her though. It will be good practice for you."

Sarah wrinkled up her snub nose and clutched me tighter. "Stupid rules," she muttered.

I felt the same. I'd had enough rules and restraints in my life already.

I hoped Sarah wasn't pressing blueberry stains into my shirt, but I didn't have the heart to push her away. Sarah whimpered against my belly.

"There, there," said Ma. "Don't make it more difficult for us all. It's time to let her go." She pulled Sarah away, allowing each of my brothers to give me a quick hug. Albair snuck in a small pinch, just to remind me nothing had changed. Pa gave me a long, gentle hug as Sarah buried her face in Ma's apron, sobbing.

"Goodbye, Pa, Goodbye Ma," I said, blinking to stop the tears from spilling.

"None of that, or you'll have us all wailing," said Ma. She quickly wiped her eyes with the back of her hand. "We have to be brave. This is the best thing that could have happened to you and we should be happy."

I forced myself to smile. Ma pulled me in for a long hug, rocking side to side. Sarah wrapped her skinny arms around our hips.

"I'm so proud of you," whispered Ma.

"I haven't done anything yet," I said.

"Oh, but you will, you will," said Ma as she released me and pulled Sarah to her side. "My lovely, bright, and good girl. You will bring honor to us all."

My family stared at me as though I had grown wings. I squirmed under the serious study of six pairs of eyes.

How was Ma going to manage without me? She already worked from dawn to dusk, and we just got by. I looked at Sarah's puffy face and drooping shoulders.

"Ma's going to need you even more while I'm away. You're going to have to work hard. Promise?"

"Promise," whispered Sarah as she wiped her nose on her sleeve.

"Just remember, if I succeed I'll have a valuable skill that will bring wealth to our family. You just have to manage for two years without me."

"I think we'll survive," said Albair. "More food for the rest of us. Less girl talk."

"I'll be older," said Sarah. "I'll be nine." She chewed on a strand of hair. "Maybe you won't recognize me when you come back."

"Only if you brush your hair." I laughed.

"I don't want you to go." Sarah rubbed the wet strand over her bottom lip back and forth like a little tail and then sucked on it.

"I'll make it up to you; I'll bring you back a present." I took the hair out of my sister's mouth. "All right?"

Sarah pouted. "No. I don't want a present. I want you."

I swallowed a lump in my throat. "In two years, you can have both." I hoped. Failure would be worse than not being selected. How much honor would that bring my mother then? The village girls would never let me forget it, especially Jenifair. I would be mocked forever.

I took a deep breath, tried to relax my twisting stomach, patted Sarah's head and said, "Be a good girl and stay out of trouble."

"I think we should be saying that to you," said Thomis. "Mind your temper."

"Yeah," said Maark. "Don't go off on the Mistresses, or they might turn you into a toad."

"Not that it wouldn't be an improvement," added Albair.

I resisted the urge to punch him. That would just prove Maark's point. Ma had told me over and over, never act with anger. Wait until your emotions are under control. I looked at my mother who was squeezing Sarah a little too tightly.

I straightened my shoulders and lifted my chin. I refused to fail. The sound of approaching horses drew our attention to the door. I put my hand on the doorknob and turned it. I would greet the Mistress and the other two girls with dignified confidence.

"Ribbit," said Albair.

V

Mistress Sangra rode up to the cottage door. She looked even more imposing astride her black horse. She trotted her own and led two mares, a brown and a grey. Two fourteen-year-old girls on horses rode behind those. One girl had short, brown hair and the other's was twisted into long black braids. They remained several paces behind the riderless horses, watching.

"May you always see clearly," I said with a small bow.

"May your vision be pure," responded Mistress Sangra. She smiled and gestured to one of the empty saddles. "The brown mare is for you to ride."

Thomis carried my bag and fastened it behind the horse's saddle.

"There you go little sister." He gave me an encouraging smile. The wind ruffled his auburn hair, the same color as mine. He formed his hands into a step and lifted me into the saddle. He gave my calf a quick pat and then stepped back.

"Thank you, Thomis." I wiggled awkwardly in the saddle, trying to find a balanced position. I did not have much experience riding. The family draft horses were used for working the fields and seldom had energy for much else.

My family lined up outside the cottage door, Ma clutching Sarah tightly in front of her, as if she was saving the child from drowning.

"The Sphere of Vision thanks you for allowing us to train your daughter," said the Mistress. "We will do our best to ensure she reaches her full potential."

Ma set Sarah aside and stepped forward. She looked up at the Mistress, her expression determined. "Take good care of my daughter," my mother said firmly.

Mistress Sangra smiled. "We will, as if she were our own."

"No," said Ma. "Not, we. I'm talking to you." She pointed at Mistress Sangra, her finger shooting out like a tiny arrow. "Any harm happens to her, I will come looking for you."

I gasped. My tiny mother, hands on her hips and a fierce expression on her face, looking up to the tall, regal Mistress on her expensive paltry. Did Ma not realize how powerful the Mistresses were?

"I understand," said Mistress Sangra with a nod. "Rest assured, Leya will be safe under my care."

The Mistress turned her mount, followed by the riderless horse. The two girls on their mares fell in behind. I turned my mare, biting my cheek to keep from laughing. My sweet little mother could still surprise me.

As my horse rounded the bend, I twisted in my saddle and waved goodbye to my family. They all waved back, except for Sarah, who had buried her face in Ma's dress.

A moment later the rider in front of me turned in her saddle. She was a short, thin girl with black hair and silver eyes. Her hair was braided and set off with small, indigo flowers. She wore fine, leather riding boots, a well-made tunic and pants, and a cloak woven in shades of cerulean, cobalt and sapphire that shimmered as she moved.

"May you always see clearly," she said.

"May your vision be pure," I responded.

"I'm Safia," said the girl in Esfera.

"Where are you from?" I asked. "I don't hear an accent."

"I am Miniria," she said.

I nodded. I thought her people were stockier. She did have the slightly slanted eyes and the tanned skin. Her people were hunters and miners. From her clothes, I guessed her family was among the wealthy mine owners. I'd heard only the poor still spoke Minirese.

"That's Caari," Safia gestured toward the sturdy, muscular girl ahead of her. "She's also from Miniria, but not my community." Caari's clothing was made of animal skins, suede and fur. Her hair was tied back with a strip of leather into a low pony tail. Would there be other Granja at the Sphere besides Mistress Sangra?

Safia's voice was high-pitched and nervous. "Caari doesn't say much. The Mistress called you Leya. Is that right?"

"Yes," I said. "Nice to meet you, Safia."

"You too." Safia turned forward, and we rode in silence.

The trail was hard packed dirt. It widened enough for two horses. I found myself riding beside the Mistress. As we travelled, I saw unfamiliar plants.

"What are these?" I asked as the trail wound through leathery-leaved shrubs with greenish-white flowers. A rabbit raced across the path in a frantic blur, pursued by a coyote, causing the horses to do a nervous dance.

"Gallberry," said Mistress Sangra. "As you see, rabbits love them."

Next, I spotted a white-tailed deer eating orange fruit. "That is a palmetto," said the Mistress. The plants varied in size and their spines were as sharp as saw teeth. I wondered if the deer were ever injured. It would take time to learn which plants were edible and

25

which poisonous in this new environment. I wondered if there were wild blueberries.

When the sun was overhead, we paused in a clearing.

"These boulders and stumps will be a good place to eat our mid-day meal," said the Mistress.

The dwarf live oak smelled like evergreens. I struggled to dismount without falling on my face. Safia slid gracefully from her horse while Caari bounded off in one smooth movement.

I hoped we didn't have to ride too far today. I was already getting sore. If I asked about it, the Mistress might think I was complaining.

Mistress Sangra opened her pack. "I have rye bread with butter, dried venison, and apples. Not a feast, but enough to hold us until we reach an inn. Leya, there is a water pouch tied to your saddle. We each have our own."

"Thank you, Mistress. I have some cheese I can share," I offered. "My mother packed some of my favorite food."

"How generous," said Mistress Sangra. She smiled. "That would be lovely."

I opened my bag and took out the bundle of white cheese. I broke off four pieces, shooed away an annoying fly, and wrapped it back up. Was it good enough for the others?

"Looks delicious," said the Mistress as I passed her a piece.

She pressed it to her nose. "Smells like my childhood."

I looked away, trying not to show my anxiety. Now that I had actually left Wren River, I felt an odd, wrenching pain.

Caari shook her head when I offered her a piece. Maybe she was homesick. Maybe she didn't like cheese. Maybe she didn't like me.

I ate the food without talking, wrestling with conflicting emotions. At home, Ma would be finished her sewing and tackling the next chore. At home, Sarah would be trying to fill my place. At home, the boys would be working in the fields. Would they talk about me? Would they tell the neighbors I had been chosen? Would people behave differently? Maybe my little sister would be treated with more dignity.

With difficulty, I swallowed the last bite of cheese. What would the food be like at the Sphere? Would they know how to make barley stew the way Ma did?

Black-eyed Caari also ate without speaking. She smelled each article of food before putting it in her mouth.

Safia glanced from Caari to me and said, "It's really good cheese. I like goat cheese too."

"We don't have a goat," I said. Our goat had died last summer and we couldn't afford another. If I succeeded, I could buy my family a whole herd of goats.

"I like caraway seeds in my cheese," said Safia. "Do you?"

I nodded even though I'd never eaten caraway. From Safia's clothes, it was apparent that she was upper class, yet she spoke to me as though we were equals.

When we stopped the second time, for a mid-afternoon break, my thighs and crotch burned from riding. I fought the urge to rub myself. How could the others stand it? My body was as stiff as a rusty pump. I walked slowly in circles.

Safia fell in beside me. "Sore?"

I paused, wondering if the girl would say something insulting. "Yes, I don't ride much." I pressed my hand to my back and stretched. No point in telling her my family's only horses were used to pull a plough.

"You look rigid, like you're having a hard time keeping your balance," said Safia.

"I'm afraid I'll fall off," I admitted as we resumed walking.

"You need to sit taller," said Safia. We sat on a grassy spot by the Mistress and Caari. "Keep your shoulders back."

I nodded. "What else?"

Safia considered. "Try to keep your feet in line with your knees. You're sticking them out sideways."

"All right." I looked at Caari who was obviously at ease on a horse. Would the girl snub me? "Any suggestions, Caari?"

"You need relax." Her Minirese accent was strong and she struggled with Esfera. "All your muscles clenched, making horse nervous. Look up and ahead. Don't keep looking down like watching horse. She knows where to put feet."

"Thanks," I said.

Caari turned away without responding. Safia looked at me. This was the most we had heard Caari speak all day.

"I've never been so far from home before," Safia whispered as the Mistress walked to her horse and searched through her pack.

"Me neither," I said. "In fact, I've never left Wren River since I've been born."

We looked expectantly at Caari who stared off into the trees without commenting.

Safia chewed on the tip of the braid that had come loose. It was a bad habit, just like Sarah's. Safia seemed younger than Caari and me. She looked like she could use a friend.

Caari stood up and walked into the woods.

"Do you know what your Vision is?" I asked Safia.

Safia twisted a strand of black hair around her finger. "No. Do you?"

"No. What's Caari's Vision, do you think?" I asked.

Safia shrugged. We both looked off toward the woods where the mysterious girl had gone.

I said, "I guess we'll find out when we get to the Sphere."

"Her eyes are black," said Safia. "It could be coal or iron."

I nodded considering all the things that were black. Maybe her Vision had something to do with bats or darkness. She seemed a mysterious girl.

"Do you know if it is your blue or green eye that is envisioned?" Safia asked.

I shrugged. "Could be either one." I wasn't going to say it might be both. That would sound like bragging and then if it didn't happen, she'd never let me forget it. "Blue could be water or sky."

"Or blueberries," said Safia.

I laughed. "Blueberries! I hope it's more than that." Then I remembered Sarah's blueberry stained face streaked with tears. Was my little sister still upset? How would she be able to sleep alone tonight? My laugh faded away. Everything felt so strange, like I didn't belong here. I couldn't even ride a horse properly. Maybe I had made the wrong choice.

VI

The fifth day we entered wetter terrain. The Mistress continued to teach me the names of the plants. Butterflies collected on the white flowers of tall, sweet bay magnolias, their honeyed-lemon smell filling the air. I picked a few egg-shaped, yellow fruits from the pond apple trees and found them passably sweet. Slowly the terrain changed.

I continued to ask for tips to improve my riding skill. During these conversations, Caari sometimes spoke. She explained how my actions affected the horse and how to keep it calm and comfortable.

Marshes lined our route on the ninth day. The Mistress pointed out coastal plain willow, bristle-tipped dahoon holly, and loblolly bay with shiny dark green leaves and yellow-centered white flowers filled the landscape. Droning bees serenaded our passing, increasing my lethargy. Cranes hunted the marshes on stilted legs. I wanted to remove my footwear and splash with them through the shallow water. They knew how to handle the heat. The surroundings became more and more alien to me the farther we travelled.

We stayed in first rate inns. I had never been inside one before, not even in Wren River. I had expected dirty floors and sticky tables from so many people coming and going. It was hard enough to get our little cottage clean with the six of us at home.

"How can they keep it clean with so many people passing through?" I asked.

"They wash the floors and wipe down the tables every night after everyone has gone to bed," said Mistress Sangra. "They air the mattresses periodically and wash the sheets weekly."

"That's a lot of work," I said.

"Yes, that is why they have such faithful customers. Masters and Mistresses stay here whenever they pass through."

The innkeepers rushed around, serving us as though we were royalty.

I was wide-eyed at the accommodations and the food, but Safia seemed to take it all for granted. The bedrooms were twice the size of my room at home. The beds had feather mattresses and fine, cotton sheets. The meals had at least four courses, not counting the bread and drink.

Mistress Sangra always rented two rooms, one for herself, and one larger one for us girls. Safia and I shared the big bed but, Caari insisted on sleeping on the floor. The innkeepers provided more blankets to accommodate her.

"Why would Mistress Sangra travel so far by herself?" Safia asked me one night as we slipped under the quilt. "A woman alone isn't really safe. Shouldn't she have guards?"

"I don't think she needs them," I answered.

"I wonder what her Vision is." Safia tucked the blankets around her feet.

"Red eyes," I said. Apples, berries, roses, fire, volcanoes?

"She must be powerful enough that no one would ever try to rob her," asked Safia.

"Possibly." I adjusted my pillow. The down feathers were incredibly soft, unlike the chicken feathers in my pillow at home. "No one would dare antagonize the Mistresses by threatening her. And, they might be afraid her Vision could bring them harm."

"It must be amazing to feel that secure," said Safia.

"Yes," I said. "To be as free as a man to do whatever you want."

"Nobody's free," muttered Caari from the floor. I giggled and cupped Safia's ear.

"She's strange," I whispered.

Safia said nothing. I guess it wasn't right to start gossiping about another Novice. Didn't Mistress Sangra say we were Vision Sisters now?

I wondered how many unusual girls I would meet at the Sphere. Perhaps they would think I was strange. Or perhaps they would find me commonplace and dull, a nobody from a little village in threadbare clothes and cheap, suede boots.

At one inn, we saw a Master. They wore robes similar to the Mistresses, but shorter. They also wore similar brooches. I wondered what task he had been asked to perform. I thought Mistress Sangra would sit and talk with him, but they barely acknowledged each other. She deliberately kept us from having any contact with him.

The next day, when we stopped for a rest, I asked the Mistress why there were fewer girls chosen each year to attend the Sphere of Vision.

The Mistress stroked her eyebrow, thinking. Then she turned to me. "Have you heard of Renegades?"

I shook my head.

"Mistresses or Masters who have become corrupt," said Safia.

"Yes," said Mistress Sangra. She looked down at the bread in her hands. "There are some who don't handle power well."

"What do they do?" I asked.

"Instead of being satisfied with the wealth, prestige, and ability to help others," answered the Mistress, "some young Masters and Mistresses have used their powers in immoral, even illegal, ways once they have left the Sphere. One yellow-eyed Master marshaled bees to attack a wealthy family in order to rob them. Several such Renegades have been hunted down, stripped of their Vision and imprisoned, or executed for their crimes."

I shivered. I did not ask how they were executed.

"We are more careful now," said Mistress Sangra. "Just because a fourteen-year-old shows Vision potential does not mean we have to fulfill it."

"What if you make a mistake?" I asked. "And you don't realize it until you're in the middle of training someone? Does that ever happen?"

The Mistress passed her hand over her face. Her voice was low. "Yes, I am sorry to say, it has. If a Novice behaves in ways that show us she is not responsible enough to be a Mistress, we stop the training and send her home. If she has developed her Vision to a point where we believe she could be a danger to others, she is stripped of her power."

"How can you do that?" I said. "I thought it was part of a person's nature?"

"It is." The Mistress massaged the bridge of her nose and then stood. "It is a horrible and dangerous thing to have to do to a person."

"Does it hurt?" asked Safia.

"Very much," said the Mistress. "But it is the best we can do for now."

"What do you mean?" asked Safia.

"In the past," said Mistress Sangra, "the Masters insisted anyone deviating from their rules should be executed. The Mistresses fought these extreme decisions, but there was little we could do. Then we realized there was another way to stop a Novice from using their Vision. But it was horrible. It was before my time, and I'm glad I never had to do it."

"Why do you care what the Masters insist?" I asked. "Don't the Mistresses make their own rules for their own Sphere?"

"I guess I should tell you some of our history," said Mistress Sangra.

"Yes, please," I said.

Mistress Sangra folded her hands in her lap and began, "Long, long ago, no one had Visions. The first to develop them were male. They banded together, and formed the first Sphere. They created the culture of the Masters of Vision and wrote the guidelines and oaths. Many years later, girls began to exhibit Visions. By this time, the Masters had earned enough money to buy an entire island. The young women were taken to the Masters' Vision Island but problems ensued, as often happens when there are many males and few females in a small area. The Masters purchased part of a second island, our island, and sat up our sanctuary under their supervision. Over the years, just as many females as males developed their Visions. We have struggled for independence and have achieved it in some areas, but not all. They still determine the punishments for oath breakers, although we have convinced them to show greater mercy. They no longer practice their hideous method for dealing with Renegades and flawed Novices."

"More horrible than stripping someone?" I asked.

"If you want to stop someone from being able to use their eyes," said the Mistress, "what would you do?"

I thought about this. Without our eyes, we cannot use our Vision. Without our eyes! I gasped and looked from Caari to Safia.

"Yes," the Mistress said. "Renegades and potential Renegades were blinded."

"Have to kill me first," said Caari.

"The Mistresses developed another way," said Mistress Sangra. "We use our powers to enter the brain and destroy the capacity for using a Vision. It is not something we want to do, but it is the least of three evils. We still continue to try to find a way that does not leave the Novice so damaged."

"Damaged?" Safia and I said together.

"Losing a part of yourself so suddenly is always damaging," she replied. "This seldom happens. If, at any time, you feel you should not fulfill your Vision, you must speak up." She looked at each of us, her face stern. "Do you understand? Don't let it go too far."

"Yes, Mistress," we all mumbled.

"If any of you do not want to continue for any reason, tell me now, and I will have you safely returned to your family."

Safia and I looked at each other. Caari crossed her arms and stared off into the trees.

That night, as I punched the pillow trying to flatten the feathers into something familiar, and closed my eyes, her words returned to me. I couldn't stop wondering how many girls were chosen, but then sent home as failures. Did their family know they were coming? Or did they just show up and have to explain why they were sent home? I'd already experienced that more than once when I still attended school in the village. I had no desire to experience it again. No matter what doubts I might have, I'd keep them to myself. I was not going home empty-handed.

During the journey, our group stopped at six other villages for Mistress Sangra to examine fourteen-year-old girls, but no one else was chosen. On an afternoon break, as I passed out the last hazel nuts from home, Safia asked, "Why did the Mistress bring four horses?"

"I think it was to carry supplies," I said.

"Not pack horse," said Caari, surprising us with a comment. She had not spoken all day.

"Mistress Prophet told me I would find four Visions," said Mistress Sangra as she passed out bread. "Eat this before we leave."

Safia blushed, realizing the Mistress had been listening.

I asked, "Then why didn't we find another girl at the other six villages?"

The Mistress chewed her bread, swallowed, and said, "Sometimes things are not as straightforward as they seem."

I looked at Safia who raised her eyebrows and shrugged with one shoulder. The Mistress smiled and then startled me with a quick wink.

It was me! I had two potentials. So Mistress Prophet thought I was two people. Mistress Sangra didn't want to embarrass me, especially since I might just be a double failure. I wiped my hands on my shirt. Didn't that mean Mistress Prophet made a mistake. What other kinds of mistakes did Mistresses make?

VII

After three weeks of travel, we arrived at the seashore. A wooden pier jutted out into the waves. The thought of crossing the ocean to an island both thrilled and terrified me. I would never be able to leave of my own accord.

I was down to my last item of clean clothing, my best green dress. Both my pants were filthy and dresses were cooler for southern travel.

I lurched off my horse and tied the reins around a royal palm tree. I'd heard of them, but never touched one before. The tree's bark was smooth but ridged. Bumpy rings circled the trunk about a hand width apart. They were so different from the firs, spruce, and poplar trees at home. They even smelled different.

Everything smelled different. I took a deep breath of warm, salty ocean breeze. I'd become accustomed to the earthy, warm hay odor of the horse, so this fresh, tropical smell was intoxicating.

I pulled off my sweaty, short boots and wiggled my toes in the warm white sand. The ocean called to me. I lifted my dress to my knees and walked into the breaking waves. I had read about the ocean, but was stunned by its immensity, beauty, and power. Vivid stripes of blue and green water, splotched with beds of dark seaweed glinted in the bright sunlight. There were small waves close to shore, and I could see rumbling rollers farther out. I released my grip on my dress and scooped up the water, taking a small sip.

"Pah!" I spit it out. "It is salty."

Mistress Sangra laughed as she tied her horse's reins. "I take it you have never been to the ocean before."

"Neither have I," said Safia as she gingerly dodged the waves and tried to touch the water with her fingers without getting her feet wet.

Caari stayed on her horse, watching.

I slowly knelt in the water enjoying the sensation on my bare legs. I lowered my body until the salty water reached my blistered and calloused inner thighs. The salt stung, but the warm water was soothing.

"You're getting your clothes all wet," said Safia.

"So," I said as I squatted further, wetting my undergarments. I bent over and splashed water on my face and neck. It stung and felt good at the same time.

Shading my eyes with my hand, I squinted into the horizon. "I can't see the island," I said.

"Vision Island II?" asked the Mistress as she stroked her horse's nose.

I nodded, scanning left and then right.

"Oh, no, dear," said Mistress Sangra. "It's too far to see from shore. Look, here comes our transport now." She pointed out to sea.

A white triangle broke the thin line of blue horizon.

"Is that a ship?" I asked as I got to my feet in the shallow water. My toes sank into the sand. A golden cloud rose over my feet and was washed away by the next wave.

"Yes, that is how we will get to the Sphere of Vision," explained Mistress Sangra.

"How did they know when to come and get us?" I asked.

"Mistress Prophet would have told them," said Mistress Sangra. "I also follow a plan for my journey so they have a fairly good idea when I'll return."

My tummy fluttered with excitement. I'd been on a canoe on Wren River, but crossing an ocean on a boat with sails!

"What 'bout the horses?" asked Caari.

"They do not like it much," said Mistress Sangra. "We blindfold them when we lead them on. They may bite or kick so we have to be careful."

"Oh," said Safia. "I don't think I can do that."

I silently agreed as I walked back to my boots. I was glad Safia felt unsure too. Mistress Sangra rode with confidence while Caari seemed to be a part of her horse.

"Don't worry. The sailors on the catamaran will lead your horses," said Mistress Sangra.

"I can do it," said Caari as she dismounted.

I dried my feet on my dress. Then I noticed Safia rebraiding her hair and tidying her clothes. I realized there might be other women from the Sphere of Vision on the boat.

I hadn't considered what kind of first impression I would make. My dress was wet and salty and now I'd dragged it through the sand. I had no other clean clothes. My hair was a sodden mess. Ma told me to think before I acted and I'd already forgotten.

The ship anchored out from shore. It was larger than anything I had ever seen and of a strange construction. A platform connected the two hulls. In between was a cabin with a large sail mounted in the middle.

"What kind of boat is that?" I asked.

"It is a catamaran ferry," said the Mistress. "It is too large to come into shore. The sailors will bring a small catamaran up to the pier. They will take one horse at a time out to the ferry and then they will come back for us."

A smaller, white, wooden catamaran powered by silver sails came to shore. Two fit women, with their hair tied back, greeted Mistress Sangra with deference. They wore baggy, grey pants, loose, white shirts and bare feet. They barely glanced at us. The taller one took the Mistress's horse, blindfolded it and led it onto the boat. Ripples of nervousness flowed over its flesh, matching the incoming waves.

"They will have to make five trips for the horses," said the Mistress. "We can all go on the sixth. You have some time to explore, if you like."

I used the opportunity to examine the beach. Seaweed was piled in ribbons along the sand, like shredded birds' nests interspersed with bits of shells, driftwood, and aquatic plants. One stiff plant was burgundy, with branches off branches off branches, the tiny ends crowned by a white pearl shaped bulb. They seemed like plants you would find in fairyland.

I picked up a handful of dry sand and let it trickle through my fingers. It was finer than salt.

Palm trees dotted the white sand. Their long trunks snaked to four times my height into six to eight large fronds. Pale, green nuts shaped like acorns, but the size of a melon, littered the ground below the palm trees. I wondered if they were edible. What would they taste like? Would we eat plants like this at the Sphere?

This was a completely different world than I had ever imagined, an exotic paradise. As nervous as I was, I was even more energized by all the wondrous things I was seeing. I had arrived in a whole new universe. I wished I could bring some of the plants home to my sister.

Caari's horse was the last to be loaded. When the sailors approached, the mare reared. Caari slipped off her back and held the reins firmly.

"S'all right," she soothed. She stroked the horse's nose as it nervously flicked its ears. "Give me blindfold," she whispered to the tall sailor.

The woman looked at Mistress Sangra, who nodded. The sailor passed the black bandana to Caari, who, continuing to talk in a calming tone, wrapped it over the nervous horse's eyes. She then passed the reins to the sailor who led the horse onto the catamaran.

Only one sailor returned for the final trip. Mistress Sangra and the three of us climbed aboard. I sat cross-legged facing the shore as the wind caught the sail and the boat surged forward with a dip and a splash. Scraps of white clouds dotted the teal, blue sky. The palm trees shushed constantly in the ocean breeze, their phthalo yellow-green fronds a thousand fingers waving goodbye. I felt as vast as the horizon.

VIII

When we reached the large catamaran, a rope ladder was dropped over the side.

"How get horses on board?" asked Caari.

"They lower a canvass sling and wrap it around the belly of the horse," said Mistress Sangra.

"They not like," said Caari as she started to climb.

"No, they don't but since there is no dock large enough for the Orca it is the best we can do."

"Orca?" I said as Caari reached the top and was helped onto the deck.

"The name of the boat," said Mistress Sangra as she motioned for Safia to climb. The girl's eyes were wide with fright. The small catamaran bumped against the hull of the larger one as waves rolled underneath. Safia stood, bent her knees trying to keep her balance, whimpered, and grabbed the first rung. The Mistress smiled encouragingly. Safia stepped onto the rope and squeaked as the boat heaved.

I followed and then the Mistress. The sailor lashed the smaller catamaran behind the boat and then climbed on board as well. The large cabin was actually a stable, with individual stalls for the horses. A walkway ran around the cabin and out onto the four points of the hulls.

"Where do people go when it rains?" I asked.

"There are rooms in the hulls below," said the Mistress. "The one on the right is for passengers."

The sailors unfurled a second sail. It snapped taut and ballooned with air. I walked to the front of one of the pontoons and leaned against the rope running along the outer edge of the boat. The wind whipped back my hair as the catamaran surged forward over the waves.

I wanted to touch the ocean again. It was exhilarating, like a second pulse but stronger, richer, and older.

Caari and Safia sat on benches farther back, under the sun shade.

"Come sit with us," said Safia. "You could fall in."

"I won't," I said as our speed increased. And if I did, it would be glorious. The blue and green water and white capped waves slid past.

"Orcas," said Mistress Sangra as she approached and pointed out to sea.

Black and white bodies broke the surface of the water in arcs. One leapt completely out of the ocean wiggling his body like a worm on a hook.

"Oh, I know about them," I said, my voice high with excitement. "They breathe like us, don't they?"

"Yes," said Mistress Sangra, holding fast to her red cloak as the wind tried to rip it away. "They are mammals."

Three creatures leapt completely out of the water, a large grin on their faces. Diamonds of water spiraled from their flukes as they flicked their tales before diving. Imitating the waves, their backs surfaced and sank, over and over.

I knew just how they felt. I had never before experienced myself so alive, weightless, and free. Water slapped against the side of the boat, waves rolled and tumbled over each other, and the clouds raced overhead.

By midday the breeze picked up. I had not left the front of the boat. I breathed deep into my belly, the ocean breeze invigorating and exciting me. The sailors lowered one sail when the catamaran tilted in a heavy wind. Ropes snapped and metal clanged.

I looked back at the others. Safia's face was white as she hung tightly onto the seat grips. Even Caari looked a little less composed.

I wouldn't leave the front of the boat. My hands gripped the rope as I rocked with the ship, my feet splayed far apart. Periodic spray wet my dress and face. I felt more alive than I ever had. The vast ocean gave me the sensation of limitlessness, I was the sea and the sea was me. I wanted to dive into the warm green-blue and swim with the orcas. I wanted to leap and twist, chatter and splash.

Dark clouds rolled in like angry fists. Thunder rumbled off in the distance. One of the horses kicked its stall and whinnied shrilly.

It was magnificent. The clouds overhead linked to the ocean, and the waves in turn linked to me. I was part of the eternal cycle of life and power and beauty. My hair whipped across my face and I laughed, loudly and with my entire body.

Lightning lit up the sky.

"I feel like I'm going to be sick," said Safia.

"Come below," said Mistress Sangra. "Caari, Leya, come below deck as well."

"I'm fine," I shouted.

"Come away now," called Mistress Sangra as she helped Safia down the stairs. "The storm is growing. We will be safer below."

My hair blew into my eyes. My wet dress slapped against my legs. The waves rumbled and rolled, white caps smashing into each other. It felt as though the ocean was surging through my body, filling me with energy and a strange exhilaration. I felt beautiful, invincible, connected to and part of everything.

"Leya!" called the Mistress.

"In a moment."

I did not want to go below into a stuffy little cabin with the other girls even though holding the rope was scraping my hands. This was where I belonged. If I had known the sea was my sister, I would have found a way to come to her sooner. My heart echoed the rhythm of the waves, my breathing matched the wind. We belonged together.

The ship rocked sharpened and my left foot slipped out from under me on the wet deck. I tightened my grip on the rope as the other foot followed. The deep, dark waves beckoned. My body was sliding, sliding—

A strong hand smacked onto my wrist as I felt myself lose control. Caari frowned as she stopped me from sliding into the ocean.

"Mistress said come now."

I swallowed and nodded. I had almost fallen overboard! Caari held my elbow tightly, pulling me across the wet deck to the stairs.

A loud crack of thunder echoed the slam of the hatch door as Caari shut it behind us. It reminded me of the slap of my angry Schoolmaster when I misbehaved.

Two benches were attached to opposite walls below with a small table between. Mistress Sangra was waiting on one bench, her face tight and her eyes narrow. Her arm was draped around Safia who was making gagging sounds and holding a bucket between her knees.

"When I tell you to move, do not ignore me." The Mistress's voice was cold as ice. "You were in more danger than you realize. If you had gone overboard, we would not be able to get you back. You would have died." She raised a finger in warning. "Then I would have had to tell your mother that I lost you before we even got to the Sphere of Visions."

"I—"

"If you are not capable of common sense at least be capable of obeying your elders."

"Yes, Mistress," I said as I lowered my head.

Would Caari tell Mistress Sangra that I had almost slipped overboard? Would the Mistress discipline me? Would that count against me as being irresponsible?

I glanced up at Mistress Sangra's scowling face. Sophia vomited, distracting her. Caari glanced at me; her lip curled. She turned away and went to sit on the other bench. I sat on the stairs, not feeling welcome on either seat.

IX

Within a few hours, the storm abated. The ferry landed at a long, wooden hinged dock that thrust far out into the blue-green ocean. The spooked horses would be released after we disembarked.

We followed Mistress Sangra down a sandy path between bushes. When we emerged into the landscaped area, the North side of the Sphere of Vision came into view. It was like nothing I had ever seen or imagined. The Mistress explained that the taupe and peach colored blocks that formed walkways and buildings were made of coral. Because of its porous and perforated quality, it was impossible to guess the age of the Sphere. I found impressions of mollusks, leaves, and fish in the blocks and wonderingly traced the ancient shapes with my fingers. Mistress Sangra waited patiently, answering questions, as our heads swiveled this way and that.

When the path divided, the Mistress turned and said, "We are going to walk along the west side of the buildings until we reach the dormitory on the south end."

There were four buildings all joined by covered walkways. We walked under one that ran along the west side of the buildings. In the spaces between, there were cultured gardens, benches, and a small pool filled with orange and gold fish.

"The first residence is where the Mistresses live," said Sangra. "There are four Mistresses here at present, myself, Mistresses Prophet, Arbor, and Denta. We all mentor at least one Novice."

We nodded in response.

"How many Novices are there?" asked Safia.

"Two Novices, twins, Minuetta and Babetta, have completed their studies but have chosen to stay a little longer and work in the infirmary. Zendra and Alise are in their second year. Mistress Denta will be bringing two new ones, according to prophecy. There are hired staff working about the place, such as in the kitchen, dormitory, stable, and grounds. You can recognize them by their clothing. They all wear white shirts and grey short pants or skirts like the women on the boat. At present, we have nine workers."

I repeated the names over and over in my head. It was a rare occurrence for me to meet someone new. All these unfamiliar names seemed a bit overwhelming.

"Here is your dormitory," said the Mistress. "The buildings to your West are the servants' dormitory and the stables and animal pens. We ask that you don't wander around there unless you're with one of us or staff."

The dormitory was stunning. Everything inside was made of white maple and mahogany. The halls were painted a fern green and had large openings allowing the sea breeze in. The rooms had slatted windows as well. The effect was calming, light, clean, and fresh.

"All the rooms are the same," said Mistress Sangra. "The only difference is the flower painted on the door. That's how you can tell who lives where."

Mine was the first. A simple sunny flower was on my door with the words Yellow Jasmine written below. Safia's, with purple bougainvillea, was across the hall, and Caari's, with pink hibiscus, was next door. Inside the entrance of my room was another tiny room with a mirror, porcelain basin and ewer with a water pump. Unlike the outhouse behind my home, the toilet was indoors and flushed.

"Where does the water come from?" I asked.

Mistress Sangra said, "There are cisterns on the roof. They collect rain water which is piped into these tanks." She pointed to the metal boxes mounted on the wall above the toilets. "To flush the toilet, you would pull the chain on the tank, opening the valve." She demonstrated.

I couldn't help it. I squealed with delight. No one in Wren River had such a thing.

"Take a few minutes to settle in," said Mistress Sangra, "and then come to the front lobby. Just follow the outside walkway we used to get here. Keep going until you run out of building then enter on the north side into the large front foyer. There, the two Novices in their second year of training, Zendra and Alise, will be waiting to orient you."

She grinned as she shut the door, enjoying my excitement.

I wondered if the second year Novices would be more like the Mistresses or us. Would they be from wealthy homes? I hoped I could make a good impression.

The bed was enormous, bigger than Ma and Pa's. The room was dark and light wood with a coral tiled floor. Most of the outside wall was window with slats to keep out sunlight during the day and night creatures at bedtime, and still allow fresh air through. I did a little dance around the room. My whole family could fit in here and not bump elbows. Sleeping alone and in such a large place, however, would take some adjustment.

I unpacked my few things and opened the large closet door. My clothing would half-fill one of the four drawers and take few hooks in the closet. I stared morosely at my worn, dirty clothing. It would have to be washed before I wore it again. Was there a river nearby or should I do it in the sink?

Before I could puzzle this out, there was a knock at the door. A man with a white shirt and grey short pants stood in the hall.

"I'm here to collect your clothes for washing." He held out a drawstring bag. "They will be returned tomorrow."

"Oh, all right, thank you," I said as I took the bag and filled it with my shabby clothing. No more beating dirty clothes on a rock with a paddle. I wondered how they washed clothes at the Sphere, but I was content to never know.

It was obvious I came from a poor family. I wondered what the hierarchy was among the Novices. Was it region of origin, class, or Vision talent that counted?

I unfolded Sarah's family picture and looked around the room. At the end of my bed was a painting of a sunset. I took it down, set it in my closet, and pressed Sarah's picture onto the nail.

I washed myself as best I could, combed and twisted my hair into a bun, and tried to wipe my best dress clean of dirt and salt stains. I waved it around the room, but even though it was hot outside, it refused to dry in the damp air. It was the one I'd worn to meet the Mistress for the first time. Maybe it would bring me good luck even though it looked bedraggled.

I was the last to arrive. Safia smiled widely when I entered, but Caari's lips were pursed and her brow was furrowed. The second year Novices wore tunics, but made of less costly materials than the Mistress's clothes. Underneath they wore loose grey pants. Their tunics did not match their eyes. They were both tall and long limbed, probably Pescan.

"Finally," said the round-cheeked girl with black eyes with a slight Pescanese accent. "May you always see clearly. I'm Zendra and this is Alise." She pointed to a girl with red flowers in her white-blonde hair. "Let's go."

"May your vision be pure. My name is Leya."

"Yeah," said Zendra with a dismissive shrug. "We were told when you arrived." She gave a long, slow look at my dress and boots. She sniffed, turned, and then walked rapidly ahead. She was

Pescan alright, probably of the merchant class not the fisherpersons.

"Welcome, Vision Sisters," said Alise as she quickly followed Zendra.

Safia gave me a wide-eyed glance and fell in line. Zendra led us across the lobby and into a hall. As we walked, Zendra carelessly pointed out the rooms with her long fingers.

"These first rooms are for classes. That's where the Mistresses will teach lessons. This one on the left is the activity room where you can learn optional things."

"Things that aren't on the curriculum," added Alise. "Just things you're interested in. I'm learning how to make jewelry."

I hoped I could learn how to ride better. Did they have a classroom for that?

"Next is the library," said Zendra. "The room on the west side is for everyone. The room on the east side is for Mistresses only. They have keys and I've never seen the inside. Apparently they keep special books about Visions and rules and stuff like that in there."

She pointed out the facilities with a bored wave of her hand. Occasionally Alise, who was almost running to keep up, would give a little more information. Safia and I nodded and tried to absorb as best we could. Caari followed, stopping when she wanted to examine something, and finally disappearing from sight.

"Where's that last girl?" asked Zendra when she eventually noticed. "Curry or whatever?"

"Her name is Caari," I said.

"So where is she?" Zendra crossed her arms and tapped her foot.

"I guess she wanted to actually see something you were pointing at," I said.

"Humph," said Zendra. She put her hands on her hips and scowled, staring back down the hall. After several minutes, she mumbled, "I thought Minirese had a better sense of direction, being hunters after all."

"Maybe she's from the mining class," said Alise.

I remembered what Mistress Sangra had said about class and region of origin being unimportant in the Sphere. Had anyone told Zendra that?

Safia gave me a worried look. Secretly, I admired Caari's refusal to rush. I wished I had thought of it.

Caari never caught up so Zendra finally continued, this time at a more reasonable pace. At the end of a hall, Zendra turned back with a grin.

"Exit here," said Zendra, "and walk along the outside of the buildings. The first one is a combination dining room, for us, and kitchen, for the servants. The wine cellar is below. We will be returning to the dining room soon since you missed supper. I guess Curry is out of luck since she decided to go on her own tour. She'll be hungry later."

"Maybe we can save her some food," whispered Safia.

"Of course," I said, and then loudly enunciated, "Her name is KAY AR EE." Although I hadn't developed any fondness for Caari on our journey, I thought I liked these girls even less.

"This building is the steam room. Anyone can use it. The laundry facilities are in the same building. Of course, I've never been in there. The building at the very back is the infirmary." She pointed to our left. "That building has the Mistress's suites. It's much nicer than our rooms. Behind that is our dormitory, you've been there."

I stopped to look at an exquisite fountain. Statues of dancing women in the center held urns over their heads from which water bubbled. How did they make water run uphill?

Zendra continued, "Further west are where the servants and animals are kept." She stopped.

I opened my mouth, but before I could speak, she said, "It's getting dark. I'll take you to get some food now."

She strode past us, and we all followed her down the walkway and into a side entrance. We entered a large room with two long tables, each able to seat a dozen people. One wall was all windows with an incredible view of the ocean. Sitting at a table, peeling an orange, was Caari. I burst out laughing.

Zendra hissed and Alise put her hand over her mouth, suppressing a giggle.

Zendra's nostrils flared as she gave Alise a look. "Come on." Her voice was cold. "Let's get the food."

They headed off to the kitchen. Safia and I joined Caari.

"How did you get here?" I asked as I pulled out a chair and took an orange. They were a rare and expensive treat in the north.

Caari grinned but did not answer. I hated when she did that.

Zendra and Alise brought bread, cheese, apples, figs, water, and sliced ham for us. They sat with us and helped themselves to the food.

"So, do you know what your Visions are?" asked Alise.

I looked at my travelling companions and then shook my head no.

"Mine is the Vision of sleep," said Zendra as she plumped her long dark curls. "I can make human and animal alike fall asleep in a second. Just like that." She snapped her fingers and then reached for an apple.

"Maybe that's what you have," said Safia to Caari. "You have black eyes too."

I paused laying slices of cheese on oat bread. I looked closer at Caari. "You know, your eyes aren't solid black. There's brown and grey. I didn't notice before. It probably isn't the Vision of sleep. It's probably something powerful." I usually wouldn't flatter her, but I wanted to give Zendra something to think about. I bit into my sandwich.

Zendra bristled. "Sleep is powerful."

Alise smiled at us. "If you ever suffer from insomnia, Zendra can help you get the rest you need. She can help those who are sick and injured, unable to sleep from pain." She poured five mugs of water.

Zendra nodded as she cut the apple into crescents.

"Oh, that is a wonderful Vision," I admitted. "You could even help teething babies to sleep and allow their Mas to rest." I remembered how difficult my sister, Sarah, had been.

"Sleep a powerful weapon," said Caari as she reached for bread and cheese.

Zendra glared at Caari. "Weapon. Why would you say that?"

"In battle," Caari pointed her knife, "make enemies' horses fall asleep. Or make enemies fall asleep. Then, kill everyone 'fore they wake."

"That's horrible!" said Zendra. She tossed her head indignantly, her curls bouncing. "I would never do that. How could you even think of such a thing?"

54

"Someone will," said Caari. She pointed her knife at Zendra. "Every Vision can help or harm, just like knife. Decide how will be used. Decide what willing do for money or power."

We exchanged uncomfortable looks.

"What's your Vision?" Safia asked delicate, pink-eyed Alise.

"I have the Vision of tongues," said the thin girl. "I can understand any spoken language and speak it in return."

"That's wondrous," said Safia.

She looked at Caari, waiting to hear how this Vision could be used to harm others. Caari looked away and took a large bite of cheese.

When we finished eating, Zendra and Alise cleaned up. "This is the one and only time we'll be doing this," said Zendra. "Starting tomorrow, everyone cleans up after herself. Fortunately, the Mistresses have hired cooks, laundresses, and cleaners so we just have to keep our rooms reasonably tidy and carry our dirty dishes to the counter by the kitchen."

She looked at me. "So, even if you are used to scrubbing pots and peeling potatoes, you don't have to here. I'm sure that will be a nice break."

She smirked as she turned with the pile of dishes. Without thinking, I shot my foot out, but then pulled it back in time. Not on my first day, but someday, Vision Sister.

X

Vegetable, fruit, and flower gardens surrounded the Sphere of Vision and, beyond that, rainforest. Cold water arrived by an underground stream. However, by following a short path through the rainforest, I could reach hot springs where the women bathed and relaxed. A thick growth of flowering shrubs and short, bushy trees encircled the springs, providing a sense of privacy.

I loved it even more than the indoor steam bath we could use during poor weather or after dark. There, a wood burning stove heated rocks. Water was tossed onto the rocks to create vapor. An adjacent tank was filled with water that absorbed the heat of the rocks. This could be scooped, mixed with cooler water from another tank, and used to wash and rinse off. I felt incredibly clean after, but it lacked the enchanting ambience of the hot springs.

After my long trip through unfamiliar country, it was in the stream that I felt most at home. Playing in Wren River had been my favorite pastime as a child. No one had to teach me how to stroke through the water; I had taken to swimming as easily as a tadpole. When I was older, and had to take the laundry to Wren River for scrubbing, I would finish with a lingering, cooling swim. Ma would scold me for taking so long but I couldn't resist.

We were given three days to rest and acclimatize while the Mistresses waited for Mistress Denta to return from her search for Novices. After our meal, I suddenly realized how exhausted I was and took full advantage of the comfortable bed.

My salt and sand stained dress was taken away the next day. The rest of my clothes were returned from the laundry. I wore my newly laundered dress, knowing I didn't appear as privileged as the others seemed to be. I was relieved on the second day when Mistress Prophet measured us three first year girls for new clothing. Soon we would all be wearing the same style of outfits, none above the other.

"All new girls get six tunics, and six pants, two each of grey, white and black," said the Mistress as she wrapped the tape measure around my thin waist. "One good white tunic and five everyday ones. What colors would you like?" She looked at me, her eerie black irises the same color as her pupils.

"How about green and blue, for each of my eyes?" I said.

The elderly woman patted my arm. "Trust me dear. If you become a full Mistress, you'll get tired of those colors. Choose something else."

I hesitated, tempted to argue. Why ask me if she wasn't going to do what I wanted? I could understand why she was tired of her robes. It would be depressing to always wear black. With her graying hair and her dark clothes, she reminded me of the somber, elderly, Widow Freya in Wren River.

"How about a lovely pink tunic," said the Mistress, "a soothing lilac, a sophisticated grey, a vibrant red, and a sunny yellow one?" She jotted down the last numbers.

I shrugged. "If you think so." It probably wasn't a good idea to get into an argument with the woman who made my clothes. Besides, they would be nicer than anything I'd ever owned. I should be grateful. I felt proud of myself for not speaking without thinking first.

Mistress Prophet returned with the completed clothing on the fourth day. They were beautiful. I was glad I hadn't been difficult for her.

"You are supposed to head to the library next," said the Mistress. "The other girls Mistress Sangra brought have already been told as well as the two that arrived late last night with Mistress Denta. Dress quickly."

I chose the fire-red tunic and black pants. The six pairs of pants were loose and soft, yet durable. Everything fit perfectly. I smiled at myself in the mirror. I no longer looked like a poor peasant girl.

I entered quietly, excited to be starting, but unsure how to behave. Safia and Caari were browsing the room. Two walls were lined with shelves filled with books. The stand-up shelves were also filled to the brim. Behind the long desk at one end was a full bookshelf encased in glass and locked. Some of the texts there looked very old. Scrolls were piled on the lowest shelf. Tables and chairs were arranged along the wall by the large windows. At the other end was an area with cushions scattered on the floor.

Mistress Sangra was sitting on a thick brown cushion with three other cushions equally spaced in front of her and two more behind those. She clapped her hands and gestured toward the empty cushions. I sat cross-legged at the back with Caari on my left, wearing a pink tunic, and Safia in front of me, in beige. I didn't want to miss a thing.

A moment later the two new girls arrived. Mistress Sangra introduced them. They both had the dark skin and pointy chins of the Caza people. Portia was a slim girl wearing a graceful, but frayed, long patterned dress worn by those in her hunter-gatherer region for special occasions. Her silvery-bright eyes reflected everything in the room.

Hydie was a plump, white-eyed girl in a shorter, patterned dress, trimmed with embroidery and fairly new. Some of the Caza people had begun to farm, but that wouldn't provide much money, as I well knew.

I guessed their Vision clothes weren't finished yet. For once I felt on par with everyone else. Hydie sat on Safia's left and Portia sat on her right.

"May you always see clearly," said Mistress Sangra. She smiled.

We gave the correct response.

"Today, I am going to start the most important lesson of your life," said the Mistress. "If you learn nothing else here, this alone will be worth the trip."

My pulse sped up. This was why I'd come. I glanced at Caari and Safia who both studied the Mistress's face.

"Sit up straight," said Mistress Sangra. "Keep your spine in a direct line to the sky. Place your hands like this." She interlocked her fingers and pressed her hands over her navel, elbows pointed slightly outward. "Now take a deep, slow breath, in and out through your nose like this."

We copied her demonstration. After several breaths, I lost my patience.

"What are—?"

"Sha!" said the Mistress. "Do not talk unless I ask you a question."

I opened my mouth to say alright, and then clamped it shut. This felt just like school and, although I liked learning new things, I hated all the sitting and waiting and listening.

"It is the mind that controls your Visions," said the Mistress. "Keep breathing as I showed you, Leya." She looked at each of us in turn. "Control your mind and you control your world."

That sort of made sense.

"Let your mind run wild, follow every impulse, and chaos will follow," continued the Mistress. "Your mind will become like the monkeys that leap from tree to tree, screeching and throwing pieces of fruit."

Monkeys! Were there wild monkeys on this island? Would I get to see them? Maybe I could make one into a pet. Maybe I could train— Darn. I hadn't heard several sentences the Mistress had spoken.

"You cannot control the mind with sheer force of will. Nor can you control it by relaxing. You can only control it with awareness. Awareness of who you are, where your thoughts arise, and how you deal with them."

I nodded. I supposed that was true, but I thought my first day would be more exciting.

"Keep still," said the Mistress.

I realized I was rocking.

"We must know ourselves before we can know the world," said Mistress Sangra. "We must know our desires, our weaknesses, our petty jealousies, our resentments, our fears, our lusts, and our hatreds."

"I don't hate anyone," I protested. Some people irritated me, but my mother said hating was like carrying a bag of rocks.

Caari gave a small sound of exasperation.

"Sorry," I muttered. Speaking of irritating. Just because she never had much to say. I adjusted my position. Perhaps if I found a comfortable spot, I could concentrate better.

Over my left shoulder, I heard Hydie's stomach emit a long gurgle. I bit my lip to keep from laughing.

"For the next four months," said the Mistress, "you will have a guided contemplation in the morning, which I expect you to repeat in the evening on your own. After that, you should be able to continue independently."

A tickle travelled across my waist. I fought the urge to scratch. We had to do this twice a day! Boring. I never liked sitting still. This must have been hard on Caari too. She seemed like an active girl. I stole a peek, but she was as immobile as a mountain.

Mistress Sangra guided us through contemplation on awareness of our breathing. It seemed to take longer than our entire trip to the Sphere of Vision.

"Now that you are in the right frame of mind," she said, "it is time to take the Oath of Vision."

XI

We were given scrolls to read while we took the oath. Caari unrolled hers upside down, glanced around, and then turned it the right way up. I realized she probably didn't know how to read. Since she also struggled to speak Esfera, this was going to be a long, difficult journey for her. I would try to be more understanding of her aloofness. She was probably more apprehensive than I was.

Fortunately, Mistress Sangra asked us to repeat after her. She recited one line at a time, waiting for us to respond in between.

"I swear to focus my energies on my study." That would be easy. I loved books and I loved learning new things.

"I will listen attentively to and obey all instruction from Masters and Mistresses." That would probably be more difficult.

"I will practice as many hours as necessary to increase my abilities." I hoped I would have time to improve my riding skills too.

"I will show respect to my mentor, teachers, and fellow students." I wondered if Zendra had taken this oath.

"My thoughts, speech, and behavior will be of the highest ethics." I was glad I hadn't tripped Zendra.

"I will never invoke my Vision in anger, deceit, avarice, or a quest for power." Oh, my, that might be difficult.

"I will use my Vision for the betterment of all. I will use my gifts with kindness and good judgment." That would make my mother proud.

"If I break this oath, may my vision be taken from me by whatever means necessary, and may I be driven from the sphere in shame and disgrace, and may all Masters, Mistresses, and Novices turn a blind eye to my suffering." A wave of nausea rolled through my stomach and I stumbled on the word blind.

Afterward, we were given books to read. Luckily, my mother had insisted I practice at home when I stopped going to school two years ago. She would be pleased to know I would now be able to put this skill to good use. She had also insisted that her children speak Esfera correctly. Sometimes villagers mocked us for speaking above our station. When I returned as a Mistress, they'd eat their words.

A little of the vocabulary in the Sphere of Vision's texts was unfamiliar. My mother had practiced reading difficult words with me using a stick and sand, and sometimes finger and flour when we were baking together. The school also let me borrow the occasional book, even though I no longer attended. Only the wealthy owned their own books.

I traced my fingers over the exquisite pictures. They seemed so real. The other girls did not seem as impressed by the illustrations. I was glad I hadn't said anything. I guess books were commonplace to them. At least I wouldn't need much help with the vocabulary, thanks to my mother's insistence that I read as well or better than other girls my age.

Quietly, Mistress Sangra drew Caari aside. A few minutes later she was taken into a private room with another Mistress. I was relieved. They knew she couldn't read.

Here I would not stand out negatively. We all had advantages and disadvantages. Soon Hydie and Portia would have clothes similar to mine; I was grateful we would all be dressed the same. Hopefully, anyone who'd seen my shabby clothes upon arrival would forget about them.

At the Sphere of Vision, I had the same chance of success as everyone else. My appearance or background would have no bearing. I was determined to master my Vision, or Visions, the quickest and with the greatest skill. Here, we all started out the same, but I was determined to finish on top.

The dining hall had three long tables with chairs. The older girls joined each other at a different table and the Mistresses ate together. There was a set of older twins who seemed inseparable, Minuetta and Babetta. They had chosen to stay longer than necessary and work in the infirmary, gathering more skills. They were both stocky, with wispy, reddish-brown hair. They were Granja, like me. They no longer participated in group lessons since they were at the stage where they focused on refining their knowledge and Visions independently. Their only difference was their eye colors. Pink-eyed Minuetta had the Vision of flesh. White-eyed Babetta had the Vision of bone. They were quiet and dignified, more like the Mistresses than the rest of us. I held them in awe and was inspired by their competence and composure. The dining hall was often the only place I saw them.

We five new girls sat together at meal time. Caari had tried to take her food out of the room but her mentor, Mistress Arbor had stopped her and said, "Meals are only to be eaten in the dining hall."

Caari ate mostly in silence. Was she just shy? Or was she embarrassed because she did not speak Esfera as well as the rest of us?

"Where are you from?" Safia asked Hydie as she passed her the pitcher of milk.

Hydie named a village in the Caza region I had never heard of, but Safia nodded.

"My father is the village baker," said Hydie.

That was why her clothes were nicer than I expected. I hadn't volunteered my background, and no one asked. Everyone knew Granja are forest and farm people. Since I had worn homespun clothes on the trip and not animal furs, it was obvious which group I belonged to and, also, since they had been outside our cottage, Safia and Caari knew we were peasant farmers. I didn't want to speak about my family or my previous life. I did not want to have to feel defensive about them.

"No one makes as good bread or cakes as my father does," said Hydie. "And the pastries, oh my. I'll miss them." She sighed and took a second slice of bread.

At the Sphere of Vision, dessert was simple, small and only served with the evening meal on occasion. The Mistresses believed sweets interfered with focus. Even so, I looked forward to the days when we received a slice of cherry pie or a bowl of peach pudding.

Hydie lowered her voice. "I'm pretty sure I know my Vision. It should be of help to my father."

I studied her white eyes. Together we said, "Flour," and then laughed.

Hydie shrugged. "That's my best guess. It might not seem like much, but my father can charge any price he wants for his baked goods and he's not envisioned. He's been hired to make wedding cakes and birth cakes for nobles and wealthy merchants for miles around." She slathered a large pat of butter on her bread. "I think I'll be able to make a pretty good living, if I'm right."

"Good thing," whispered Zendra as she passed the table. "As big as you are, I don't imagine you'll have many suitors."

I cursed. "Don't listen to her. She's just nasty."

Hydie set her bread down on her plate. "She's probably right."

"The only man Zendra will ever catch has to be deaf," I said. "She never says anything worth hearing yet she never stops flapping her big mouth."

Hydie laughed and picked up her bread.

"She won't even have to use her eyes to activate her Vision," I said. "She just has to start talking, and it will happen."

"What is her Vision?" asked Portia.

"Sleep," I said.

Hydie giggled and took a bite of the bread.

"I'm surprised Zendra hasn't been sent home," said Portia. "For a second year Novice, she doesn't seem to have the right attitude."

"Do they send people home for the wrong attitude?" I looked from one to the other.

"Oh, sure," said Portia. "There was another girl in Zendra's group. She was from my village. She was sent home after a month. No one knows for sure why, but rumor says it was because she was argumentative."

"Oh." I chewed on my lip and glanced at the table of Mistresses. Mistress Sangra met my eye and gave a small nod. I twitched and then nodded back. Sometimes it seemed as though that woman could read my mind.

"Zendra never behaves badly in front of the Mistresses," said Safia. "She projects the perfect image whenever they're around. I don't think they have a clue how mean she is to the other girls. It's unfortunate."

"Too bad none of the Mistresses have the Vision of truth," said Portia. "Then she'd be seen for what she really is."

Portia looked at Safia. "Do you think our Visions are the same? We both have silver eyes."

We looked from one to the other.

"They aren't exactly the same," said Hydie.

I nodded. "Portia's are brighter, almost white sometimes. They seem to change depending on what you're looking at."

"Like a mirror," said Hydie.

"Yeah, that's right." I wished we all knew our potentials and whether we would fulfill them. "I hope we don't have to wait much longer to find out. That's why we're here, isn't it. What about you, Caari? Do you know what your Vision is?"

Caari wiped her mouth on her sleeve, stood up, and carried away her dishes.

"She sure doesn't talk much," said Safia.

For the hundredth time, I wondered why the girl didn't seem to trust us.

XII

The next day Mistress Sangra lectured on awareness of the workings of our bodies. The day after was focused on detaching ourselves from random thoughts. Recognizing ego driven desires followed that. I was always the last to arrive, dreading the lessons. I kept waiting for something interesting to happen, and when it didn't, my mind wandered.

By the end of the first week, I tuned out Mistress Sangra's voice more and more often and lost myself in daydreams. I really didn't see any value in all that introspective stuff. It was like when Ma used to sit me on a chair in the corner and tell me to think about what I had done wrong. I wasn't five years old anymore.

Just when I was on the verge of complaining, Mistress Sangra announced, "Individual lessons begin on developing your Visions tomorrow. You each have been assigned a private mentor."

It was about time. I hadn't come all this way to learn how to sit quietly.

Mistress Sangra was my mentor. She smiled and explained, "How better to keep my promise to your mother." I liked Mistress Sangra, but I hoped the private tutoring would be more interesting than the group work.

The next day we met in the flower garden and sat side by side on a stone bench. A plover flew past. Its white hood and black belly reminded me of Freya, the oldest woman in Wren River village, with her long white hair and black widow dresses. A stab of homesickness made me flinch.

Mistress Sangra pointed out pink and salmon-colored hibiscus and bright red, pompom zinnias. We didn't grow flowers at home. All our land was used to grow food.

I wanted to get down to why I had come. If I had to leave Ma shorthanded, it needed to be worthwhile.

"Is it permissible to ask what your Vision is?" I asked as I studied the Mistress's red eyes.

"It is the Vision of blood," said the Mistress.

I shivered. "And the other three Mistresses? Can I know theirs as well?"

"Mistress Denta has the Vision of Teeth and medicine, Mistress Arbor has the Vision of Wood, and Mistress Prophet has the Vision of prophecy. But, her greatest asset is the Power of The Veil."

"The Veil?"

"There is only one Mistress who has it. It is passed to the next recipient at her death. The Masters have tried for generations to access it. They have searched through their own Novices for the potential. But, so far it only comes to a female. This does not make Masters of the Sphere very happy."

"What does The Veil do?" I asked.

"At the Mistress's will," she said, "it creates a protective invisible bubble around her and those near her. It cannot be breached by fist, knife, arrow, water, or flame."

"That's some power."

"It is a sacred trust used only to help subdue Renegade Mistresses when needed. Mistress Prophet is getting too old for long trips and battles with lawbreakers. I hope she is not called again."

She stood and gestured to me to walk with her along the path made of broken pieces of peach-colored coral. "Let us walk for a bit. I spend too much time each day sitting."

"Of course," I said, "so do I."

The Mistress continued, "I can cure weaknesses and diseases of the blood, dissolve clots, stop internal hemorrhaging, and stem bleeding."

"Wow," I said, "that's wonderful." I thought of Caari and the way she saw both sides of a Vision, good and bad. What kind of weapon could this be? Blood clots, hemorrhaging… I shivered.

"Cold?" asked Mistress Sangra.

"No, I'm fine." I glanced away, hoping my dismay did not show on my face. "What's my Vision?"

"Unfortunately, you are both blessed and challenged." Mistress Sangra paused to step over a small salamander as it darted into the path. "Those with two different colored eyes are, very rarely, able to master double Visions. However, more often, neither eye is powerful enough alone. Then, neither Vision is mastered. However, your Visions may be harmonious, not like fire and water."

"What are they?" I tried to keep the impatience out of my voice.

"I think you know one of them." The Mistress grinned. "I've watched you swimming. And there was your compulsion on the ship. You must have sensed your affinity by now."

I smiled. Rivers, brooks, ponds, and now the ocean all called to me, each playing their own siren song. The babble of a stream over rounded stones, the quiet lapping of pond water against the reeds, the wild toss and churn of the river, and the changeable expanse of a cold, green-blue ocean spoke to my soul. I was never more at peace than when I floated on the surface of

Wren River, sounds muffled and distorted by the water in my ears, ushering me into a quiet world. While my siblings loved tart apple juice or frothy milk, I always preferred cool spring water to quench my thirst. When others rushed indoors when it rained, I rushed out. The drops tattooed my skin like a thousand joyful fingers as I raised my face to the clouds.

"It's water," I said.

The Mistress nodded. "Only you will know for certain when you begin training, but I suspect it is so." Mistress Sangra stopped to snap off two small clusters of yellow flowers. "This is ixora." She passed one to me. She pulled out each stamen and sucked the nectar, then dropped the spent blossom back into the flower bed.

"What if it isn't water?" I said as I copied her. The nectar was sweet as honey.

"Then we try other things," said my mentor as she plucked a hot pink flower. "Bougainvillea," she said as she tucked it into her long, loose brown and grey hair, "but usually it is something you have already felt comfortable with. Of course, we can never be sure what, if any, Vision will be fulfilled."

"You mean I might go home with nothing?" I said.

"Yes, I am sorry. There are no guarantees. However, you would not go home with nothing. You will keep the clothes we have given you and all the things you have learned and experienced."

We continued walking. It didn't seem like much for all this disruption to my family.

I asked, "How do you even know I have a Vision? All you did was stare into my eyes."

"It is part of my gift. I can 'see' into the blood vessels behind the eyes. Those with a Vision are different inside."

"Can only those with the Vision of blood assess potentials?" I asked.

"There are other women with different Visions than mine who could do it. Healing, seeing through the eyes of another, mind control—"

I jerked to a shocked stop. "Mind control! People can do that?"

Mistress Sangra stopped and turned to me. "Some rare people could. If you are interested in the history of the Visions and the Sphere, the librarian will help you find the information you want."

"I think I will," I said.

"We have no Mistress of Water at the Sphere at the moment," said Mistress Sangra, as she resumed walking, "so I cannot show you exactly what to do. All I can do is demonstrate how I call upon my own Vision. That will be all you need. You will discover for yourself your connection to water and how that can be utilized."

We reached another stone bench surrounded by white and mauve flower clusters each crowned with bright yellow centers. Mistress Sangra named them gaindass, and then sat and patted the bench for me to join her.

"While the power seems to come from our eyes, they are useless without the mind," said the Mistress. "Unless you can control your thoughts, your Visions will not manifest."

I nodded and took a deep breath. This would be harder than I had anticipated. I often spoke or acted without thinking. I often did not know what my thoughts were. Contemplating did nothing but make me feel more restless.

"It is extremely difficult, if not impossible, for ordinary people to block all thought. We can learn to focus our thoughts, and let the distractions fall away. Can you visualize people and places in your mind?"

I closed my eyes and thought of home. "I can see my little sister holding my mother's skirt."

"Can you see the details? Describe them." The Mistress's voice was quiet and soothing.

"She has a tiny button nose," I said.

"Can you actually see it, or are you just remembering that it is so?"

I focused on my sister's face. "Her eyes were red from crying. Her nose was a little sunburned. She had blueberry stains on her lips."

"Good," said Mistress Sangra, "now open your eyes and see her."

I opened my eyes. "That's a lot harder. All the flowers push away my image of her."

"I want you to practice," said my mentor. "When you can keep the image of your sister's face no matter what you are looking at, hold it for as long as possible. Start with only opening your eyes very slightly and work your way up to wide open. I have tasks to do. Stay here and practice until meal time. Do not allow yourself to be distracted. Meet me here tomorrow at the same time and bring a bucket of water."

"All right," I said. I watched Mistress Sangra walk away, her lovely robe swaying with each step.

I sighed and concentrated on my sister's face. There it was, the cute little nose and the blueberry stains. I wondered how many berries Sarah ate and how many she put in the basket. Probably not enough for a single pie. Oops, I wasn't concentrating. All right, Sarah's face. A little sunburned nose. Sarah should have been wearing her hat. Ma was forever scolding her for leaving it somewhere. Just like she leaves other—dang! Concentrate.

I worked until I heard the mealtime bell being struck. I felt frustrated, disappointed, and mentally exhausted. If I couldn't even do something this simple, how was I ever going to do the harder things? I stood and stretched.

If they realized my mind leapt around like a frog, would they find another method to teach me or just send me home? The village girls would laugh themselves silly. I could imagine the new nicknames they would devise. Washout. Failure. They already called me Loser Leya. If the Mistresses tried to send me back, I would throw myself off the ship and let the ocean drag me to the bottom.

XIII

The water was cold and clear when I filled the tin bucket from the pump. Mistress Sangra waited for me on the bench.

"Set it on the ground in front of us," said my mentor.

I did. I smoothed my pink tunic and joined Mistress Sangra on the bench.

"Now, close your eyes and imagine the water in the bucket splashing."

I did. Water moving, droplets flying into the air.

"Can you see it clearly?" The Mistress spoke quietly.

"I think so, Mistress."

"Good. Open your eyes and look at the bucket. You must have a clear line of sight to whatever you are acting upon."

I opened my eyes. The bucket looked the same as it had before. Nothing happened. I turned my head to look at my mentor. Mistress Sangra gently pushed my chin with her fingertips, turning me back toward the bucket.

"Now, envision the splashes, as though you are looking at the bucket through a window on which you have painted splashes. Focus your mind on the painting and allow the actual bucket image to blur in the background. Keep focusing on the picture of the splashes, give it color. Make it real."

I concentrated with my eyes wide open. I remembered the babbling brook not far from home. I thought of the white-capped waves on the ocean crossing. I remembered splashing my brothers as we swam in the river. Each time I tried to create a frozen picture of the moving water. For a few seconds, I could hold the image of the water splashing, but then it would fade and be replaced by the water in the bucket, reflecting the cloudy sky in its placid surface. The pictures switched back and forth.

"I don't think it's working," I said.

"It is only the first part," said Mistress Sangra. "Now, think about the sensations attached to the water splashing. What does it sound like? How does it move? Can you smell the water? Make the painting shift."

My thoughts were jumbled. The tropical salty smell of the ocean. The woodsy cold smell of the brook in the forest. The smell of crayfish and yellow lilies in the pond. Sharp slaps of my hand against surface water and the swoosh of the splash. The deep surging rhythm of the ocean. The hyper dance of the river over smooth egg-like stones. I tried to sort them, tried to attach them to the stubborn water sitting motionless in the bucket.

"I don't understand. Nothing is happening!" I couldn't control the rise in my voice.

"Patience, my dear. Nothing worthwhile comes easily."

I huffed with exasperation. I clenched my fists and glared at the bucket, willing the water to splash. I didn't blink. I didn't move. I barely breathed. Damn it, move, move, stupid water. Move! Nothing happened.

I swallowed a lump forming in my throat. What if I couldn't do it? The image wavered and disappeared. I thought of Ma's face filled with disappointment.

"I failed," I whispered.

"You have not failed until you quit trying. Perhaps that is enough for today," said Mistress Sangra. "Practice every day. I will see you in a week." She patted my hand. "Do not expect instant success. I am not worried. You need not be either. I sense a strength in you that makes me believe you will succeed." She stood and brushed off her robe. As she walked away, she said, "Keep practicing."

Practice what? Drying out my eyeballs staring at a stupid bucket. Damn it. I sank my face into my hands, covering my eyes. Useless eyes. I wasn't special. Just a freak like the blacksmith's cat. At least he could catch mice.

I lowered my hands, sat up straight, and gritted my teeth. I fought an urge to jump up and kick the bucket into the flowers, sending the water in a cascading arc. I hated that bucket. Hated the way it sat there defiantly. I wanted to throw it across the garden. I gave it a spiteful glare, imagining it flying through the air.

My eyes burned with pain. The water jumped. "I did it!" I screamed as I leapt to my feet. I looked around the garden. Mistress Sangra was gone. No one was in sight. The pain faded from my eyes. I sat down again and stared at the stupid bucket.

"I sort of did it, anyway." I took a deep breath and slowed my heart beat. I remembered Ma's warning not to act with anger. But, anger had made the water move. I couldn't very well make myself angry whenever I wanted to use my Vision. Water was the Vision of life, a peaceful Vision. There had to be another way to invoke it.

Caari's tunics were shades of brown, beige, and grey. At mealtime, I asked her how she had obtained them in her eye colors. She shrugged.

"Did you make a fuss?" I asked, "to get the colors you wanted?"

She looked at me as though I'd grown another head. She didn't seem all that interested in how she looked. Her knees were often smudged with dirt and the tunics wrinkled. I doubt anyone commented on it. She kept to herself, not interested in the other Novices. At least she snubbed us all equally.

Safia, though, quickly became my closest friend. I was small for my age, so she was a head taller. She didn't have much confidence, even though she got along with everyone and always seemed to know the right thing to say. With her long black hair and silver eyes, she seemed older than her years.

A few days after my success with the bucket, Portia offered to share her Vision with us. Hydie, Safia, and I followed her into the library. Zendra and Alise were reading at a table by the window.

Zendra's curly hair was pinned back with bejeweled clasps, but messy strands had broken free. She was never as tidy as I expected. Now we had to wear our clothing for two days before sending it to the laundry. Zendra's were horribly wrinkled on the second day. I think she came from a home with servants and never had to do her own hair or care for her own clothes before. She probably threw them on the floor at night. Maybe that's why she was so comfortable giving orders and saying whatever she wanted.

Alise was friendly to us whenever Zendra wasn't around. I think she could have become our friend if she hadn't been caught in Zendra's web the previous year. Alise seemed too afraid to oppose her.

"Everyone get a book to read," whispered Portia.

"What kind of book?" asked Safia.

"It doesn't matter. You're not going to read it."

"But you just said—"

"Camouflage, you ninny," said Portia. "I'm going to play a trick on Zendra."

"Oh," said Safia. She looked over at the other table. "I just remembered I had something I have to do." She scurried out the door.

"Any other cowards want to abandon ship?" asked Portia.

I grinned. "Not me."

"Count me in," said Hydie.

The three of us brought books to a table where we could clearly see Zendra.

"I have the Vision of Reflection," said Portia. "I can imitate people."

We nodded.

"I've pretty much mastered my gift already. In fact, I'm one of the lucky few that does not have to have the person or object I am imitating in view. If I see and hear it once, I can remember."

Hydie and I exchanged wide-eyed looks. Mistress Sangra said I needed to see the water to act upon it, and I was having trouble doing that. Portia must have amazing talent.

"Try not to stare at Zendra," Portia said as she poked Hydie. "Act like you're reading."

"Oops, sorry," Hydie said.

Portia cleared her throat and said, "Zendra, would you please come here for a minute?" but the voice came from the hallway and sounded exactly like Mistress Prophet.

Zendra looked up, set down her book, and stood.

"Quickly, please," said Portia, again from the hallway.

Zendra smoothed down her tunic, plastered a smile on her face, and went out to the doorway. We watched her look left and then right.

"Mistress?" she said.

She waited a few moments, and then came back in with a puzzled look on her face. She shrugged, sat down, and picked up her book.

"Zendra!" Portia said. "Did you not hear me ask you to come here?"

Zendra jumped up, dropping her book, and hurried into the hall. Hydie giggled. I covered my mouth to keep from laughing. Zendra walked down the hall to the left, and then she returned and walked down the hall to the right. Hydie was snorting with suppressed laughter.

Zendra came back into the room and glared at us. "I don't know how you did that," she said, "but I know it was you peasants."

My blood rose.

Hydie burst out laughing. Zendra's face reddened.

"Laugh it up, girls," she said. "Don't think I'll forget this."

XIV

I seldom saw the oldest Novices, Minuetta and Babetta, and then usually just at mealtimes. One day they joined the Mistresses at their table.

"Look," I whispered and gestured with a sideways head tilt. "Where the twins are sitting."

"Mistress Denta said we can sit wherever we want," said Hydie. "There are no prescribed divisions."

Mistress Denta was Hydie's mentor.

"Then why don't you ever sit with her?" I asked.

"No thanks," said Hydie. "I think I'd be too nervous to eat." She looked at each of us and covered her mouth with her hand. "Oh, my. I'm glad Zendra isn't sitting with us. She'd never let that comment go by."

"She's a witch," I said. "I don't know why anyone sits with her."

The Sphere of Vision ran by routine. Together, all the Novices studied reading, writing, mathematics, history, geography, ethics, politics, and science. Caari was often taken out when it came to independent reading. I had expected Zendra to say something to her, but she never did. Perhaps Caari's calm, steely stare unnerved her.

One day we were studying maps, learning the different regions and cities within our boundary.

"Who can tell me what direction the Master's Sphere of Vision is from here?" asked Mistress Denta. She looked hopefully at Caari who stared at the map and refused to meet the Mistress's white eyes. "Caari?"

Caari shrugged and slumped in her seat.

"This is a very important skill for a Mistress," said Mistress Denta. "She often has to travel to new places on her own. It wouldn't do to be late or get lost."

Safia and I picked up our line sticks and placed them on our maps, trying to determine the direction. Portia gave the map a quick glance and smiled. She was often given advanced lessons with the older girls. Her parents had provided her with private tutors and her knowledge was extensive.

"I'd just hire a guide," said Zendra as she frowned at her line stick.

"They aren't always available," said the Mistress. "Besides, it isn't wise to put your safety completely in the hands of a stranger. You should have some idea of where you are going even with a guide."

"I got it," said Alise.

Zendra glared at her.

Alise blinked and bit her lip. "Would you like me to help you, Zendra?"

Zendra pasted on a sweet smile and said, "Yes, please."

Alise went to her side of the table.

A little later, Mistress Denta asked a question about Willow Bend, a northern city we had just found on the map.

"I need to leave for a moment," she said. "While I'm gone, discuss the source of this city's wealth." She picked a paper up off her desk and left.

"Silk," answered Hydie.

"Silk!" said Zendra. "Of course not. That's only made in the south. Right Alise?"

"Um, I'm not sure," said Alise. "I know silkworms eat mulberry leaves."

I wondered what kind of berry Alise and Zendra had used to make their lips so red.

"You're both sort of right," said Hydie. "Willow Bend has bred a northern variety of orange tree the silkworms will eat as well. You can feel a slight difference in the cloth."

"That's right," said Portia. "I had a red dress made from Willow Bend silk. It felt almost as light as southern silk but was more durable."

"Mulberry silk is much better quality," Zendra said. "That's what I use to wipe my fat ass."

I gasped. Then I realized Zendra's lips hadn't move. The voice continued.

"I say this because I want everyone to know how rich and important I was before I came to the Sphere. Here, I'm less than ordinary, but I like to pretend I'm—"

"Shut up, Portia!" Zendra jumped up, her fists clenched. "I know it's you doing that."

"Whatever are you talking about?" said Portia, her face a picture of innocence.

Hydie laughed loudly. I chuckled and then saw Safia's frown.

"I want everyone to pay attention to me," continued Portia in Zendra's voice. "Me, me, and only me. I am the center of the—"

"What is happening here?" said Mistress Denta as she walked in the door.

Zendra looked at her and then placed her hands over her face, sobbing. I suspect there were no actual tears, but the ruse worked.

"Portia is imitating my voice and saying terribly vulgar things about me," cried Zendra.

"It's almost time to stop," said Mistress Denta. "Everyone is dismissed except Zendra and Portia.

Safia left. Hydie and I waited in the hall for Portia while Alise waited for Zendra. None of us spoke.

A while later they emerged. Portia's face was pale and Zendra was grinning from ear to ear.

Alise smiled at her, but Zendra grabbed her arm, "Thanks so much for making me look stupid about the silk in Willow Bend."

"I'm sorry," said Alise. "I didn't mean to."

As Hydie, Portia, and I walked by, Zendra turned to Hydie and said, "So, do people eat the oranges from the silkworm trees?"

"Oh," said Hydie. "I don't really know."

"Well, how about that. Something about food the kitchen girl doesn't know. I'm sure people can't eat them then. If they were edible, you'd be sure to have eaten them. Many, many of them."

I took Hydie's arm. "Ignore her," I said. Then I looked at Zendra. My eyes narrowed and my lips pressed tightly together. "You too, Portia. Come on. Don't give her what she wants – a reaction."

Hydie relaxed her lips, puffed out her cheeks, and blew out a long breath. Then she took Portia's other arm. We walked down the hall, our heads high. I was proud of my composure.

Portia never told us what the Mistress said but, after that, she didn't smile much and she wrinkled her nose whenever she saw a Mistress. Zendra should have left it between us girls. She had no right to drag in the Mistresses. What Portia did to her was nothing compared to Zendra's relentless nastiness to Hydie. The Sphere of Vision wasn't much different than Wren River. The rich had done whatever they like and everyone else had to bend to them.

XV

Each day for three hours in the morning and two hours in the afternoon, we worked in the classroom, sometimes the library, with different teachers. Once I realized the books held stories of incredible women and adventures in places I had never seen, I became a voracious reader.

Occasionally, we would be taken outdoors to gather botany specimens. Caari came to life during this time; enclosed spaces made her shrink and mute. Outside, she was full of questions and just as many answers. When discussing animals, she was the expert.

I, too, found myself drawn to the gardens, woods, and fields. But I also enjoyed thumbing through the library books to learn the names and qualities of vegetation and how they were best grown. I was determined to bring seeds and clippings of some of the hardier plants home to Wren River.

Sometimes we new girls discussed our progress, or lack of advancement.

"I'm getting better control over the movement of water," I said as we walked toward the dining hall. "Now I can make a decent splash in the bucket. I'm able to push through the pain and it actually seems to lessen the more I practice. I do have to rest in between efforts, but my recovery time is improving as well."

"Mistress Sangra wrapped two spoons in cloth and put one in each of my hands. It took me two weeks to be able to tell which one was a silver spoon," said Safia with a sigh. "The other was a wooden one. I still cannot tell if they are set on a table in front of me."

"It'll come," I said as I patted my friend's arm. "I'm not doing much better. What about you, Caari? You already seemed to have a Vision with animals as far as I could tell."

Caari grinned. "'Tis a sacred trust to have so much power over them now, but I aim to use it carefully. One of the goats broke a leg the other day. I kept it still while Babetta worked on it. I visit every day and keep it calm so it don't reinjure itself 'fore it's healed completely."

"That's wonderful," I said. All I could do was make water splash in a bucket. Wasn't that fabulous?

"Where's Lumpy?" asked Zendra as she walked in front of us. "I can't believe she is going to be late for a meal."

"There is no one at the Sphere by that name," I said. I reached out to pinch her, hard. Safia intercepted my hand and pulled it back.

"Yeah, okay. Hydie then."

"She left early to help in the kitchen," said Safia. "She's trying out a new biscuit."

Hydie spent many hours there and everyone reaped the benefit. The Mistresses exclaimed over her creations with flour.

"Why is she even here?" asked Zendra as we entered the dining hall. "She can bake. Big deal. Send her home to be an apprentice."

"There's more to it," said Safia. "She's learning how to enrich the flour, make it more nutritious, but also light at the same time. And she has plans to make it last a long time without spoiling."

We walked over to the buffet table.

"Who cares?" said Zendra. She wrinkled her nose at the smell of fish.

"Everyone," I said as I reached for a piece of fish. I passed it slowly in front of Zendra before putting it on my plate. "If the Mistresses have their way, they'll never let her leave. I think even thin Mistress Sangra has filled out a little."

Zendra snorted. "Great, so we'll all be as fat as Lumpy."

The sixth week, when the first year girls sat together for lunch, we watched Alise and Zendra sit at another table. Zendra steadily avoided sitting with us and whenever Alise was too friendly, Zendra would snap her invisible leash and make her fall in step. As usual, Caari took her food outside. I didn't know how she had managed it, but she had been given permission to eat one meal a day outdoors.

"What snobs," I said. "Why doesn't anyone sit with us?"

"I don't think Caari can stand to be indoors another minute," said Safia.

Hydie nodded. "She looks like she's ready to jump out the window by the third hour of lessons."

"I know," I said. "That's fine. She's not that comfortable speaking Esfera. Besides, she's not social with anyone else, human anyway."

"Yeah," said Hydie. "I don't take it as personally as when Alise and Zendra won't talk to me. Will we be that snobbish next year?"

"Babetta and Minuetta always greet me when we pass," said Safia.

We nodded.

Hydie waved hopefully as Alise glanced our way. Alise quickly looked back to Zendra and whispered something. Zendra glanced over her shoulder at us and grimaced.

"They make me feel like something they stepped in while walking through the barn," said Hydie as she took a sip of water. She lifted the mug too quickly and a bit of water splashed on her chin. She wiped it with the back of her hand.

I watched Zendra, my irritation bubbling below the surface. "They should be trying to encourage younger Novices. I wonder if the Mistresses realize how disdainful they are of us. Maybe their awareness contemplation should be centered on respect for others."

"I think Alise might be friendlier if she wasn't such a puppet of Zendra's," said Safia. "Zendra is always so assertive. It's a little intimidating. She never doubts herself."

"She acts like she's more important than the rest of us," said Portia. "She's always putting on airs. Even her table manners are impeccable."

I grinned. "Impeccable, eh? When I say now, watch them."

Hydie nodded and shifted her body to have a better view.

Zendra munched on grapes while Alise spread butter on oat bread. Chatting away, Zendra reached for the mug of water. She paused in her conversation and lifted the mug toward her lips.

"Now," I whispered.

Just as the mug touched Zendra's lips, the water gushed out, flooding her face, wetting her curls, and going up her nose. She dropped the mug and jumped up, coughing and wiping her face, her hair dripping.

"Look away," I ordered.

"I can't," said Hydie. "It's just too beautiful a sight."

Zendra wiped the water from her tunic, looking around the room in embarrassment. She paused at the table where Hydie and I sat, grinning. Hydie winked. Zendra's eyes widened. She looked at me, but I just continued eating.

Portia giggled and resumed eating her lunch. "Aren't you worried Zendra will make you fall asleep in the middle of class?"

"It would be pretty obvious she did it if I suddenly collapsed in the middle of geometry. We're not supposed to use our Visions foolishly and a second year Novice would be expected to know that and abide by the rule."

"Not a first year Novice though?" asked Safia with one eyebrow raised.

"I don't know what you mean," I said. "Zendra was too busy talking to pay attention to what she was doing."

"Right." Hydie grinned. "I think you're my hero. That'll show her not to ignore us."

I wasn't sure if that was a good thing.

XVI

"Well done," said Mistress Sangra as she watched me splash the water high out of the bucket, hold it suspended in the air for a few seconds, and then let it fall onto the grass. We sat on the usual bench in the garden.

"You must learn to master the direction the water flows, how fast, and how much. Too much can be dangerous, too little useless. Fast can cause erosion or damage and slow might be too late if there is an emergency. Controlling how much is vital."

"Yes, Mistress," I said as I shrank inside.

"Refine, refine, refine." Mistress Sangra held her pointer finger and thumb far apart and slowly brought them closer together. "Your awareness contemplation will help you with control as well."

I flinched. Three times I had fallen asleep during morning group contemplations. I'd stayed up reading the nights before. There was so much to read and the Sphere's books were one of a kind. Whenever this happened, I glared at Zendra, but the girl continued breathing deeply with her eyes closed. The Mistress had scolded me and told me to start going to bed earlier. It would not do for Mistress Sangra to suspect that I was not doing my evening contemplations in addition to dozing off inappropriately. I meant to. I would just start reading and suddenly it was far past the time I could keep my eyes open. Surely learning about the world was more important. I could contemplate for hours when I finished my training.

The Mistress continued. "Every molecule must be completely under your direction. It is vital that it never get out of control. Not enough control can be disastrous."

It took several weeks to develop that finesse. Finally, I could separate a single drop from the rest and leave it hanging on the edge of the bucket. I could explode all the water upward like a geyser. Remembering my trick on Zendra, I felt a twinge of guilt. I had little control then and was lucky I hadn't driven the water into the girl's lungs. I could have killed Zendra and it would have been obvious I had done it. Was there a death penalty for Novices who accidentally killed with their Visions? I vowed to never be so impulsive again.

Mistress Sangra praised my progress and told me I would next learn how to purify water.

At last I could do something really useful. I couldn't imagine ever needing to make water jump out from a bucket, but removing the parasites and contaminants, now that was a valuable skill. Maybe that would be easier to do now that I had mastered some of my Vision.

The next lesson outside, the day was overcast with clouds and an intermittent cold wind blew. I wore a new grey woolen cloak against the chill. It had been left on my bed the day before. I guess Mistress Prophet predicted cold weather.

I sat, cross-legged on the sand, in front of my mentor. Mistress Sangra sat on a rotting log near the slow river's edge. My stomach was a nervous flutter, but the chatter of the river soothed me, much like listening to my parents talk after I had gone to bed.

"One of the most important skills is learning how to purify water with a touch. That can save the lives of an entire village whose water has become contaminated. Water is the basis of all life. Your Vision is sacred. A holy trust. You must treat it with dignity and use it with honor."

Had Alise told the Mistress of my prank against Zendra? Wouldn't I have been sent home in shame? But then, they couldn't prove it wasn't an accident caused by Zendra's own hands. I cursed myself for such a foolish impulse. It could have cost me everything.

Mistress Sangra passed me a bucket. "Fill it with water from the river."

I walked to the river's edge. I was beginning to hate that stupid bucket. Defeated by a piece of tin. Augh!

A pale blue and soft brown rail ran through the reeds at the water's edge. I watched the bird's skinny legs dash here and there. I touched the water with my finger tips. It was cold. Did birds get cold feet? I would have to look that up in the library.

I scooped out the water, watching the droplets run down the bucket's metal side and drip into the sand. Straightening my shoulders, I walked back to the Mistress and set the bucket at her feet. Mistress Sangra spat into the bucket. Using a small stick, she then scraped fungus from the fallen tree and stirred it into the water.

"Now," the Mistress said. "Purify it."

"How?" I asked.

"You must see its purity in your mind's eye. Just as you do when you make the water splash."

I closed my eyes and concentrated.

"No, dear, you have to keep your eyes open. You know how to do that now. Most Vision Mistresses must be looking at what they are trying to control. There are a few who can see something, or someone, once and be able to act upon it for ever after."

"Like Portia?"

"Yes. In our books, as well, there are records of a rare few who could act upon people they have never seen by touching an item they have touched. I've never known anyone like that myself and find the thought of that much power a little alarming."

"My eyes get tired," I said.

"I know it is difficult with two different eyes," said Mistress Sangra. "Your green eye will see the water as it is, but your blue eye, through your mind, must envision it pure down to the last molecule. Think about what you have learned in science."

I nodded, took a deep slow breath and stared at the water. I tried to imagine the water clear and pure. Slowly a second image overlapped the first. As it strengthened, I felt sweat form on my brow.

"That is right," coaxed Mistress Sangra. "Hold the image in your mind. Now, believe in its reality. Make that image the true one."

I trembled with effort. Nothing changed. I closed my eyes, exhausted.

"It's too hard," I said. "Maybe I can get a job with troubadours making water do tricks."

Mistress Sangra laughed. I blushed.

"Are you sure that is worthy of your talent?" asked the Mistress. "Take a look."

Slowly I spread my fingers and peaked through at the bucket. I gave a small cry of joy and lowered my hands. "It's clean! I did it! I did it!"

"Indeed it is." Mistress Sangra smiled broadly. "I do not expect Novices to succeed at something so difficult on their first try."

"What else can I do?" I asked, wiggling.

"With water? Whatever you can envision. Your mind is your canvas and the water is your paint."

94

I was going to try everything. I would read what other Water Mistresses could do and try it all. I would become unstoppable. I would be famous. People would clamor for my talent, pay any price. I would pick and choose who to help.

Daily, I practiced purifying my drinking water. I found an underground stream and diverted the water to the surface, although I was careful to return it to its natural course. When it rained, I made the puddles dance like fountains.

"Be careful not to accidentally bring harm with your Vision," said Mistress Sangra. "Every action must be carefully considered for its consequences. If you summon a cloud and make it rain, that means the place that would have received that water, does not. Mistresses of Water in the past were able to make it pour by crying. You might try that when the gardens are dry. Remember, though, every Mistress must use her Vision with great care. Altering the natural order can have grave consequences. Think before you act."

When I wasn't reading or practicing, I was swimming. The ocean was my second heart. I had always loved swimming in Wren River when women weren't washing laundry in it or men weren't cleaning fish. The ocean was never cold and it was filled with endless wonders.

At first the salty water stung my eyes so I kept them tightly closed when I submerged. One afternoon, I felt something brush my hand and opened my eyes in surprise. A long streak of greenish-yellow flashed by. I flipped my body around, watching the eel swim away. It had a lengthy fin on its back and its skin was wrinkled and cracked. It stared back at me with its cold bluish eyes. What teeth were hidden in its long snout? Cautiously, I swam backwards to shore, watching it the whole time.

As I stumbled out of the water, my vision blurred. I blinked. It cleared and then it blurred again. I rubbed my eyes. The lids felt heavy. No, it couldn't be. Something was wrong with my eyes.

XVII

I headed for the infirmary, my chest tight with fear. Had I damaged my eyes from too much swimming in salt water? Surely the Mistresses would have warned me. Could a blind Mistress still control her vision? By the time I reached the infirmary, I had succumbed to tears.

"May you always see clearly," I sobbed when Mistress Denta opened to my knock. "But I can't. I can't."

"May your vision be pure. What is it, my dear?" she asked as she took my arm and steered me inside.

"My eyes, there's something wrong with my eyes. They feel heavy and my vision keeps blurring."

"Come in," she said. "Sit here." She led me to a chair as she swept back her white robe. She pulled another chair up in front of mine.

I wiped my eyes on my sleeve. I told her what had happened in the ocean.

The Mistress took a candle and waved it back and forth in front of me studying my eyes. I found hers unnerving; the iris being the same color as the white around it. Her black pupils seemed like two tiny holes.

"Hmm. Interesting." She put down the candle.

"What is it?" I asked.

"I don't think there's anything wrong," said Mistress Denta as she patted my hand. "However, I want to try an experiment based on what you have told me."

She filled a basin with water, set it on a high table, and then poured in a scoop of salt. She dropped a coin into the bottom of the basin.

"I want you to submerge your face in the water," she said, "then open your eyes and read what it says on the coin."

"I can't do that," I said. "The salt will sting. I'll harm my eyes even more."

"Trust me, dear. I will rinse your eyes immediately if it does."

I walked to the basin. I could see salt collecting on the white bottom. I took a deep breath, bent over and pressed my face into the water. I forced my eyes to open. A copper coin came into focus. I lifted my face out of the basin. Mistress Denta grabbed my cheeks and stared into my eyes. My vision blurred. I blinked and then it cleared. I dried my face on a towel the Mistress provided.

"It had PAX on the coin," I said.

Mistress Denta stared at me. "How remarkable."

I tilted my head. "I don't know why the salt didn't burn."

"Because it never touched your eyeball."

"But I opened my eyes."

"Your outward eyelids, yes." She reached over, placed one hand on the back of my head to hold me steady, and then tugged on my eyelid with her fingers.

"Pardon?"

"Do you know how frogs can see under water?" She released me and leaned back.

I shook my head, bewildered.

"They have a second set of eyelids," the Mistress said. "They are transparent. They protect the eyeball yet allow the frog to see underwater."

"I understand," I said. Then I touched my eyelid. "You mean?"

"Yes, you have grown a second set of eyelids for seeing under water. They are not visible until you use them and barely even then."

"Oh, no. I'm a freak. Like my ugly, crooked teeth aren't enough to deal with."

Mistress Denta laughed. "Honey, haven't you realized, we are all freaks here. The freakier, the better. If you want straight teeth, I can do that for you."

"Really? Yes, yes please!"

"And, don't worry. I can't tell you have a second set of eyelids by just looking."

"I guess I over-reacted."

"I can't straighten your teeth all at once," said the Mistress. "It would be far too painful. Even what I'm about to do will make you sore for a few days."

She poured a foul-smelling green liquid into a tiny cup and passed it to me.

"Swish this over your teeth for as long as you can, and then swallow it."

I did. My mouth felt numb. She had me lie back on the cot and open my mouth. As she stared at my teeth, I felt them shift and move. It bled a little.

"Come back once a week," she said. "It will take several sessions to put them into correct alignment."

When I returned to my room, there was a letter on my bed from Sarah. She corresponded for the whole family about once a month. I decided not to tell them about my eyes. I would wait and see if anyone noticed. My teeth, however, were another story. I couldn't stop smiling in the mirror. I could already see a difference.

I soon learned to love my special eyelids as well. Under the water, I could see as clearly as above. I watched the way the sun sparkled on the waves, and then broke through the water to form shimmering strings of light on the sandy bottom. Thin, fat, spread out, bunched, rolled over each other, the sunlight endlessly danced in ribbons of gold.

I swam far out from shore to the coral reef and spent hours examining the fantastical formations and the fish and sea creatures that lived there. When I tired, I would lie on my back and will the waves to carry me to shore.

One sunny afternoon, Safia and I were wading in the fresh water river that emptied into the ocean. Tiny fish darted about our feet like silver darning needles. Safia was giggling and occasionally splashing me with water. She wore her long black hair twisted into a knot on top of her head.

As I flicked water into my friend's face, I wondered if Safia realized I could call the river to drench her. That would be cheating and mean. I laughed and clumsily chased Safia along the pebbly shallows, scooping water and flinging it toward her.

"Simple is as simple does," said Zendra as she entered the beach area from a trail.

"What are you doing here?" I said, standing still. "I didn't think you were the outdoors type."

"Within reason," said Zendra as she pushed back a curl and tucked it behind her ear.

"Are you coming wading with us?" asked Safia.

"Hardly," said Zendra. "I was here yesterday with Alise. Sometimes I just have to indulge her whims. I lost a silver necklace, and I think it was here."

She looked at Safia. "Why don't you make yourself useful and see if you can locate it?"

"Safia is not your servant," I snapped.

"No, it's alright," said Safia. "I'll be glad to help if I can."

She walked up and down the shore looking into the water. Zendra waited on shore, her arms crossed and her lips pursed. After a few minutes, she removed her shoes and rolled up her pants.

"I had better do it myself," she said. "You aren't getting anywhere. Obviously your Vision isn't working."

She knocked Safia to the side as she stepped into the water. Safia lost her balance and fell backwards, hard, water soaking her tunic from neckline to bottom.

"Ow!" she cried.

I rushed over to help her up. Safia rubbed her left buttock.

"That really hurt."

"It's not my fault you're so clumsy," said Zendra as she searched.

I helped Safia to shore. I set my friend down on a sparse thatch of grass and then turned back to watch Zendra. What a nasty witch. That snob thought she could treat others like trash. The sooner she was gone, the better.

XVIII

Zendra walked further into the water, rolling her pants up to above her knees. I focused on the river. The surge of water flowed through me. The river slowed, the level dropped as I pushed the water upstream and toward the other bank.

Zendra looked over her shoulder at me.

"I thought lowering the water might help you locate it," I said. "Find the stupid necklace and get out of here."

Zendra made an ugly face, turned away, and walked a bit farther from shore.

"Hurry up," I said. "I can't hold it forever."

Zendra waved me away with a dismissive gesture.

"I'm not kidding," I said. "Hurry up."

I felt my strength wavering as she continued to wade through the water.

"Times up," I said. "Come back."

"In a minute," said Zendra.

I lost control. The river resumed its natural course in a high rush. Zendra screamed, flailed her arms and fell sideways. She crawled along the shore spitting and splashing, trying to get to her feet as the water rose. The altered current towed her into the middle of the river.

"Help!" cried Zendra as she slipped below the surface.

I bent over laughing, but Safia stumbled to her feet and said, "I don't think she can swim."

I gulped. I watched as Zendra's face bobbed into view further downstream and then disappeared below the water again. I tried to command the water to hold Zendra up, but nothing happened.

"Damn," I said as I raced into the river.

I was a strong swimmer and quickly reached her. Zendra was barely able to push herself to the surface and gasp a breath before she sank again. I thought a drowning person would be screaming for help, but then I realized Zendra needed every second on the surface to breathe. She went down deeper just as I reached her. I dove.

Her eyes wide with panic, Zendra wrapped her arms around me and tried to climb over me to the surface. Her nails dug into my neck and she kneed me in the chin in her desperate struggle for air. I commanded the water to hold us both up. This time it obeyed.

"You're fine," I yelled. "I won't let you drown."

Zendra gasped and coughed, unable to speak, clinging to me as the water carried us to shore. She collapsed in the shallows, crawled to land, and flopped on to her side, coughing and whimpering. I stood over her watching nervously. Once she had caught her breath, Zendra moaned and held her stomach.

A moment later, Safia arrived, out of breath from running along the shore.

"Is she alright?" she asked.

"She's fine," I said, forcing my voice to be calm and nonchalant even though my heart was pounding. "She just swallowed a little water."

"You tried to kill me," whimpered Zendra, as she sat up and pushed her hair out of her face. Her curls were now transformed into dark, dripping, wavy strands.

"Don't be melodramatic," I said. "I told you to hurry up. If I wanted to drown you, you'd be dead. I was trying to help."

"Liar!" said Zendra as she stumbled to her feet. "You're a menace." She pushed me in the chest. "Don't think I don't know what you did with the mug of water." She paused to catch her breath, her hand pressed against her throat.

"I don't—" I began.

"Shut up! You think you are so superior to the rest of us," snapped Zendra.

"What?"

"Mistress Sangra's favorite girl. You won't be her favorite for much longer."

She stumbled back along the beach in the direction of her shoes. She glanced back once over her shoulder and screamed, "I hate you! You're going to pay for this!"

Safia bit her lip as she looked at me.

"You know it was an accident, don't you?" I said.

Safia looked away. "If you say so," she whispered. "I'd better make sure she's all right." She quickly followed Zendra down the path.

Mistress Sangra summoned me to the classroom. Zendra was in the infirmary for observation. Near drowning victims sometimes inhale water that later causes lung failure. Safia was leaving the room as I approached.

I grabbed my friend's sleeve. "What did the Mistress ask you?"

"She asked me what happened," said Safia, avoiding my eyes.

"What did you say?"

Safia tugged her sleeve away. "The truth."

The door opened. Mistress Sangra said, "Come in please, Leya." Safia hurried away.

The Mistress shut the door behind us. She stood in front of me, looking down. I had not felt so vulnerable since my selection in the clearing near Wren River.

"I don't believe you tried to kill Zendra," said the Mistress.

"Of course not!"

"Sha. Don't talk unless you are asked a question."

I nodded.

"Did you use your powers in anger with the deliberate aim of bringing harm to another?"

"No! Even if she deserved a dunking —" I clamped my mouth shut.

"This is deeply worrisome. You may have broken your oath. The Spheres of Vision are dealing more severely with this kind of behavior, and rightly so." The Mistress turned and walked toward her chair. She sat down, sighed, and looked up at me. "If a Mistress indulges her personal vendettas, she is nothing but a criminal. It is the same as using a weapon to harm another. Worse."

"I'm sorry, Mistress," I blurted. "I told her to come to shore. My eyes were searing with pain. She wouldn't listen. I just wanted her to find the stupid necklace and get out of there. She was being mean to Safia. I don't think you realize how awful she is to the other girls."

"So you did this for your friend?" The Mistress frowned.

"Yes."

"And how would Safia have felt if Zendra died on her behalf?'

I licked my lips. "It wasn't like that. I didn't try to hurt her." I hadn't even considered how all this would have affected my gentle, sensitive friend.

"Were you teaching Zendra a lesson by being careless with her safety?" She crossed her arms.

"That's not what I intended," I said.

"And there was no personal anger, no desire to punish, no joy in seeing her suffer."

I dropped my eyes and did not answer. The Mistress sighed.

"At least you didn't try to lie."

"I swear I didn't know she couldn't swim. I never would have risked putting her in deep water even if she could. I told her I couldn't hold it for long. It was an accident." My voice shook.

"An accident." Mistress Sangra echoed me as she tapped the desk top with her fingernails. "Are you saying you have no control over your Vision? Why did you offer to hold the water then? Offering to do something when you can't control the outcome is worse than not offering at all."

I sniffled while she paused.

"Do you remember swearing, ' I will use my gifts with kindness and good judgment.' when you took the oath? If you are going to take such risks, perhaps you should not have a Vision. Perhaps, we should remove it. Then there will be no more accidents." She stressed the last word.

I put my hands over my face and sobbed. I was so ashamed. "Maybe you should," I said. "Maybe I don't deserve the Vision. I was careless. I could have killed her. It's just luck that I'm a good swimmer."

Mistress Sangra did not respond. The only sound for a few moments was my sobbing.

"We also told Zendra's mother she would be safe at the Sphere of Vision. Now the girl no longer feels safe." The Mistress stood, walked to the window, and looked out into the garden. "Zendra will return home with a tale of her life being endangered by another Novice. How comfortable will mothers in the future feel sending their children here?"

"Oh, Mistress. I am so sorry." I clenched my fists as tears ran down my face.

"We have figured out that Zendra is not the sweetest young woman at the Sphere," said Mistress Sangra. "We are trying to teach her to be more respectful. However, she has only used words to harm others. If she ever were to use her Vision, then she would be dealt with severely. As anyone would."

"I will apologize to Zendra," I said, "and try to make her understand that it was my fault, not the Sphere's. I'll do whatever it takes to calm her."

"That would be a good start," said the Mistress. "I will be meeting with the other Mistresses to decide your punishment and your future. In the meantime, perhaps you should lengthen your evening contemplations. You need to recognize your anger and its triggers. You need to learn how to defuse it without losing control. You must not allow your emotion to make you impetuous."

I stared at her feet, hoping the Mistress would not figure out that I didn't do the evening contemplations.

"I will," I said. "I promise." I meant it when I said it.

XIX

I was put on laundry duty for a month. I had to wash and iron Zendra's clothes personally and deliver them to her twice a week. It was the most humiliating punishment they could have given me.

The first time I knocked on the door, she opened it and immediately turned away.

"May you always see clearly. I've come for your laundry," I said.

Zendra was already walking to her closet. She reached it, pulled out the laundry bag, and dragged it across the floor by the strings. When she reached the doorway, she picked it up, flung it into my chest, making me stagger backward, and slammed the door.

I returned the next day with the clothes neatly folded. I carried the laundry bag over one shoulder and the clothes in both arms. When I knocked, Zendra opened the door, grabbed the clothes, and slammed the door shut without looking at me.

"I still have the laundry bag," I called.

No answer. I knocked. "Zendra, I have the laundry bag."

There was still no response so I hooked it over the door handle and left.

I thought Zendra would lord it over me, but the girl never spoke to me again.

Portia and Hydie watched me carefully. Their conversations were short and polite. I learned they had told the Mistresses about Zendra's bullying. She was given extra counseling but she had never crossed the line by using her Vision inappropriately.

I think the girls thought I had dunked Zendra deliberately. They seemed uncomfortable around me. It was lonelier than when I first arrived.

Minuetta and Babetta still smiled and said hello, but we only ever exchanged a few words. The day before they were to leave, we had our longest conversation.

I was returning from the beach and had arrived at the bottom of the back stairs. Hydie emerged from the building and was about to take the first step down, when I said in my friendliest voice, "May you always see clearly."

I must have surprised her. Her head jerked up and then she stumbled. Her foot landed crookedly on the top step and she lost her balance. Down the stairs she tumbled. I raced up the steps, and caught her half way, but the damage was done.

"My shoulder!" she cried as I held her.

She was twisted into an odd position on the steps, her face white with shock. Her collarbone had broken and the bone protruded through the skin. Blood oozed down her tunic.

"Oh, Hydie," I said, and sat down beside her.

Hydie's breathing changed to small gasps. "It's bad."

"Are you going to faint?" I asked. "Should I help you to the bottom of the stairs?"

"No, no, I don't want to move." Her eyes filled with tears.

"Should I go get someone? But, I don't want to leave you on the stairs in case you faint and fall the rest of the way." Part of me wanted to run and part of me thought I should stay. I helped her lay is flat as possible.

"I'll be all right for a bit," said Hydie.

I ran into the building screaming like a mad woman. "Help, help, we need help."

Babetta and Minuetta rushed down the hall.

"What is it?" asked Babetta, her white eyes wide.

"Hydie has fallen on the stairs and her collarbone is broken. The bone is sticking out through the skin and she's bleeding and she's all alone."

Babetta came with me and Minuetta went for a Mistress.

Under Mistress Denta's supervision, they loaded Hydie on a stretcher and headed for the infirmary. Hydie moaned. I took her hand and walked along beside her.

"Hang on, Hydie," I said. "We're almost there."

She shoved my hand away. I stepped back, disappointed, but she suddenly leaned over the side of the stretcher and vomited. Minuetta, who was carrying the rear of the stretcher, stepped over it and kept going.

"Leya," Hydie moaned and reached for my hand. I scurried forward and took hers.

In the infirmary, Mistress Denta gave her something for the pain from a small flask. Within minutes, Hydie's face relaxed, and her breathing eased. It must have been strong medicine.

Working together, under Mistress Denta's instruction, Babetta healed the bone and Minuetta healed the flesh. Hydie held my hand until they were finished.

"We'll let her sleep now," said Mistress Denta as Hydie's eyes closed. "It's not completely healed. Only time will do that."

"Should I stay with her?" I asked.

"I'll be in the next room," said Mistress Denta.

I gently tucked Hydie's hand under the sheet.

"I'm alright now," Hydie whispered.

Minuetta and Babetta exchanged smiles. We all headed for the exit.

"Leya," Hydie said.

I turned back. "Yes?"

"Thank you for being such a good friend. I'm glad you were here."

"You're welcome," I said.

Babetta and Minuetta's Visions shortened Hydie's convalescence from weeks to days. They were gentle and reassuring, calling her Little Sister.

I contemplated about it that night. I felt doubly ashamed for the way I had used my Vision. Those girls understood their responsibility better than I ever had. I also felt relieved that Hydie had forgiven me. I was grateful I had had the chance to help. I wondered if I had caused the accident by startling her. I wondered if I should be ashamed for having a part of me feeling glad. Having a Vision was more complex than I had ever imagined.

XX

I did the required evening contemplations from then on, although I did not double it as the Mistress suggested. I just couldn't force myself to sit that long. I thought that if I did it the way I was supposed to in the beginning, everything would fall into place. I set aside the same time every day. As soon as the sun went down, I sat for the originally prescribed time period. It was difficult to focus as I was often thinking about the book I was reading and couldn't wait to get back to it.

At the end of the month, Mistress Sangra called me to her office and asked me what I had learned about myself. This time she allowed me to sit as we talked.

I explained that my biggest trigger was a sense of injustice, but I also realized that this was based on judgment of others, often when I did not have enough information to make a clear conclusion. I hated the judgmental natures of girls like Jenifair and Zendra, but I had been just like them. I reminded myself daily that my Vision was for helping others, not punishing them.

"There were Mistresses who thought you should be stripped of your Vision," said Mistress Sangra, "but I spoke on your behalf."

"Why?" I asked.

"Because you admitted that maybe you should lose your Vision. You confessed your carelessness and you were truly ashamed. I believe this experience will make you more cautious and respectful of the power you have."

"It will Mistress," I said. "I never want to have anyone fear me the way my friends did afterward. Even Safia has been distant. I don't think she trusts me anymore."

The Mistress nodded. "Then you will have to work hard to regain that trust, if it is possible."

"I will."

"Do you understand that knowledge without wisdom is dangerous? Power without wisdom, doubly dangerous?"

"Yes Mistress. I'll think before I act from now on, I promise."

"A wise man once said, 'To conquer others is no great accomplishment. True strength and courage is shown when one can conquer oneself.' Do you understand?"

I nodded. I thought I did, but I was wrong.

XXI

Since Safia spent less time with me, and Zendra and Alise avoided me, I thought I should give another shot at befriending Caari. I really knew nothing about her. Maybe I could even help her improve her reading, if she wanted me to. I didn't know if Caari was aware of what had happened with Zendra. If she was, she never brought it up.

Caari's Vision was with black, brown, and grey beasts, both tame and wild. Since infancy, she had a special affinity to animals. With training, she could now call the birds from the sky, calm the wildest animal, and coax the fish to jump into her net. Hers was a powerful Vision and she trusted no one, but herself, to use it wisely.

One evening, I met her in the library. Caari was carrying a small text to a table. "May you always see clearly," I said. "I don't see you here very often."

Caari looked up. "May your vision be pure. I guess you noticed I'm more of an outdoors person." She set the text down and pulled out a chair.

I laughed. "I think I got that. I hope this is okay to say, but your Esfera has really improved."

"Thanks. I've been listening carefully."

"Don't be afraid to talk more, though," I said.

Caari grinned. "I'm not much of a talker, even in Minirese."

"What are you reading?" I asked.

"I thought I'd see if there were others with similar Visions to me and what they did with it," said Caari.

"Me too," I said. "I'm learning a lot about my abilities."

"Yeah," said Caari. "I don't want to repeat other people's mistakes."

I sighed. "I guess. I make enough original mistakes."

Caari laughed loudly. I smiled.

I said, "It doesn't hurt to find out what previous Mistresses were hired for either. It's thrilling to know how valuable we've become. People will pay a great deal for us to bring them what they want."

"Humans have done enough harm to animals," she said. "I'll not put my Vision up for sale so rich nobles can slaughter more deer."

"Oh," I said. "Good for you. Well, I hope you find something interesting and useful in the book."

Caari nodded as she sat and pulled her chair in to the table. I wandered off to browse. My Vision was now progressing faster than if I had depended solely on Mistress Sangra's teaching. These old stories inspired me to experiment in ways I wouldn't have imagined.

I found where the staff hung wet laundry on the clothes line, pulled the water from its threads in a slow stream, and dried the fabrics in minutes. It was a mundane activity, but I found these little things delightful. What a difference it would make to my mother not to depend on the vagaries of weather.

I discovered other Water Mistresses cut apples and bananas into slices and removed the water. The dried fruit would last for weeks. They could also quick dry strips of meat. That would be helpful for travelling and preserving food for winter.

Twice, Caari took me horseback riding. I realized I had learned a lot on the trip to the Sphere. By keeping the ride to a reasonable length of time, I managed to truly enjoy myself.

Caari taught me how to brush down the horse and clean his hooves afterward.

"Isn't this a job for the stable man?" I asked.

"It is a way to thank the horse," said Caari. "To show respect for him. And to teach him to trust you."

"Makes sense," I said.

After we finished, I told her, "I think doing that will help me be less tense around the horse."

"Good," said Caari.

After the ride, I went to Safia's room. My friend was stitching an embroidered table cloth. I sat on the bed, watching her, wondering why Safia wasn't spending her time practicing her Vision. However, I didn't mention it, hoping that our relationship was returning to normal, and not wanting to spoil it. Safia offered information on her own.

"My Vision should have enabled me to find silver ore deep below the surface of the earth, but it's not working out that way. I should have been able to tell how deep it ran and how much was there. I just can't seem to master it."

"That's too bad," I said.

"Mistress Sangra says if I can find a silver spoon hidden in the room, I should be able to work my way up to finding mineral deposits." Safia shrugged. "I'm not sure I want to. My parents were thrilled when I was picked, but I would rather have stayed home. I guess I don't have enough ambition. I prefer a simple life. I don't really see how my Vision could be of genuine help to others."

"I'm sure you could put your Vision to good use," I said.

"Yeah, if anyone wants to find a lost silver button." Safia snorted and went back to sewing.

This Vision could have made her wealthy beyond her imaginings; she would be able to ask any price for her services. I didn't understand why she didn't try harder.

Periodically, Novices were sent, with a Mistress, to villages on nearby islands that needed their assistance. I was thrilled to have more opportunities to be on the ocean. I begged the sailors to let me help and learned how to tack into the wind, raise and lower the sails, and keep the craft steady. Aware of every movement of the sea, I was quickly able to navigate and control the boat like an expert.

A village on a nearby island held a monthly market. Here I shopped for jewelry and gifts for my family. The Sphere also sent coins to my parents in Wren River as recompense for taking a productive member away for two years.

Caari seldom came on these trips, and then only to buy something for one of the animals. She was not interested in jewelry or trinkets.

After one expedition, Portia was red-faced on the return trip. She hunched down in the seat and stared at the deck.

"Are you ill?" I asked.

"No one is to speak to Portia right now," said Mistress Denta. Her voice was firm.

I looked at Portia. She glanced up and her eyes met mine. They were bloodshot from crying. She hugged herself and looked back at her feet.

Once ashore, Mistress Denta hustled Portia away, never releasing her arm. Hydie approached me as we walked down the path. Her face was pale.

"What happened?" I whispered as we walked toward the Sphere.

"She was using her Vision of Reflection to trick the vendors so she could steal," said Hydie.

"What? There must be a mistake."

"I saw them catch her," said Hydie. "The vendors made her empty her bag. It was stuffed with jewelry, scarves, and candy she stole. They said someone had been stealing from them for quite a while, but they hadn't suspected a Novice."

"Oh, no, what will the Mistresses do?"

"I don't know," said Hydie. "She's already been in trouble a couple of times since that incident in the classroom with Zendra."

"I didn't know."

"I didn't want to gossip about her," said Hydie. "But that isn't the worst of it."

I wanted to cover my ears.

"When the merchants were chasing her," said Heidi, "she used her Vision to steer them in the wrong direction. One of them was trampled by a coach and is badly hurt. The Mistresses are treating him in the village. He couldn't be moved."

"Oh no," I said. "Do you think they'll send her home?"

Hydie nodded. "Or worse. She broke the oath. She caused injury to another. They will say she can no longer be trusted with her Vision."

XXII

The Mistresses searched Portia's room and found a hoard of stolen items. Why did she think no one would notice? We were only given a little money to spend, and the cleaning staff might have seen her treasure.

She was confined to her room while the Mistresses decided her fate. A few days later, a Master arrived on the island. He had the face of the storm cloud. His robes were dark grey.

That evening Safia shared with me in my room what she had learned about the strange Master.

"His name is Raze," she said. He has the power of selective destruction. He can zero in on part of the building and turn it to ash."

"Why is he here?" I asked.

Sophia chewed on the end of her braid. "He can also destroy a part of a person's body."

I thought about that and then jumped up from my bed. "Like eyes?"

Safia nodded. "But I think he can be more subtle than that."

"Why did they bring him here?" I paced back and forth. "Why don't the Mistresses handle their own problems?"

"Any breach of the oath must be brought to the attention of the Masters," said Safia. "The Mistresses will be punished if they don't keep the Masters informed."

I stopped pacing. "Did they tell him about me?"

"I don't think so," said Safia. "They believed it was an accident."

"It was an accident," I said staring at Safia.

She nodded. "I know."

"Is he going to decide what happens to Portia?"

Safia shrugged. Whatever he was here for did not bode well for our friend.

I had trouble sleeping that night. I couldn't get thoughts of Portia out of my mind. She would have to do more than laundry duty for what she had done. The reputation of the Sphere of Vision had been damaged. Stealing wasn't an impulse of temper. It was well thought out, and she had done it more than once.

I decided some fresh air would do me good. The moon was full, so I slipped into my darkest clothes and went outside. I could hear the ocean off in the distance and the night birds calling. A small frog flopped across the coral stones. I took a deep breath of fresh air. Watching the waves would soothe me. I headed down the path to the shore. Halfway down, I heard voices coming from the dark.

I might be in trouble for wandering around at night if a Mistress caught me. There were wolves and large wild cats in the jungle that were bolder under dark. We had been warned not to venture away from the buildings. I quickly turned back. A horrifying scream stopped me dead. Was someone being attacked?

She screamed again. "Stop, stop, please, it hurts, it hurts."

My brain said run for help, but my body turned and raced down the path to the shore. That voice was familiar. When I reached the beach, I looked right, and then left. Two torches stuck in the sand illuminated four figures. A smaller figure was tied to a palm tree.

"Please, don't do this," begged the prisoner. "I'll be good. I swear."

It was Portia. I opened my mouth to scream for her release, but stopped when I heard Mistress Sangra respond. I crouched down, hiding behind a cat's claw creeper, and watched. I strained to hear over the crashing waves. Slowly, I crept on all fours down the beach, hugging the bird's nest anthurium as I went. Torchlight played over red, white, and brown robes.

"You have left us no choice, Portia," said Mistress Sangra. "Try to relax. We will do it as quickly as we can."

"No, no, no, no." Each no became louder and higher.

"You have broken your oath," said a male figure in black. Master Raze! Of course.

The Master and the three Mistresses pressed closely in around Portia. What were they doing to her? She screamed a cry so full of pain, I had to cover my ears. My hands were shaking. I knew I should leave, but I felt I had to stay. I had to be my Vision Sister's witness. The screams seemed to go on and on, but it was probably only a minute or two. The ocean responded to my terror, waves rolling in higher and faster. At the end, Portia sobbed brokenly.

"There, there," said Mistress Sangra. "It is over now."

Two of the Mistresses stepped back as one untied her. Mistress Sangra caught Portia as she fell to her knees. The one in white unhooked a flask from her belt. What had they done? Was this some kind of ritual abuse? Who should I tell? Would anyone believe me?

"Drink this," said a woman. It sounded like Mistress Denta. Her voice was gentle and soothing, the way she spoke to a patient in the infirmary. "It will stop the pain."

She held something to Portia's lips. I wondered if it was what she had given Hydie for the broken collarbone.

They helped Portia to her feet and turned in my direction.

"I have her," said Master Raze.

"No," said Mistress Sangra. "You've done enough. We will care for her from here on."

On all fours, I crawled to the path and then ran all the way back to my room. When I clicked my door shut, I leaned against the inside, trying to catch my breath. Tears rolled down my cheeks as the sound of Portia's screams echoed in my mind. I hadn't heard her speak after. How badly was she damaged?

The next morning, I hid outside the infirmary. A short while later, Mistress Arbor and Mistress Sangra went inside. They emerged half-carrying Portia between them with Mistress Denta following. Portia sagged and seemed unable to control her feet properly. Her head bobbed on her shoulders like a flower with a broken stem.

I snuck down to the pier. They carried Portia onto the catamaran. Mistress Denta gave one of the sailors a flask and spoke to her for a while. Mistress Sangra gave her a small money bag. When the sailors began the launch, the three Mistresses turned and headed back to the Sphere. I pulled back farther into the bird's nest anthurium and watched them pass. As Mistress Sangra wiped her eyes, Mistress Arbor reached out and squeezed her arm in a comforting gesture.

We were told Portia had been stripped of her Vision and sent home. No questions were allowed. I told no one what I had seen, but I would never forget Portia's slack face.

I became even more determined to expand my Vision as far as it would go. If the Mistresses came for me, I would fight. I would call the ocean to rise up and flood the Sphere. I would bring the rain so thick lightning would follow. They would not find me an easy target.

As my skills increased, I helped people locate the best dig sites for wells and purified contaminated water. It was thrilling to know the difference my Vision made in the lives of the communities. I began to understand how my Ma felt when she helped sew a quilt for a newly married couple and brought food to the ill.

I ached to do something dramatic with my talent, something to prove myself unique and indispensable. In the Sphere Chronicles was a story of a previous Mistress of Water who had saved an entire city from flooding. How would that feel, to hold back tons of water, creating a dam long enough for the water to be diverted safely away from homes and people? What strength that would take! How the people would cheer. No one would allow a Vision to be stripped from such a heroine.

What was I thinking? I should not wish fear and danger on others just so that I could make myself more secure. That was as bad as using it to punish people.

I needed to return home and have my brothers treat me like their annoying sister again. I should be seeing things clearly by now, but I was more confused than ever. I must remember that it was the Vision that was awesome, not me.

Alise and Zendra finished their studies and returned to their villages. Since the water incident, Zendra had avoided me and was apprehensive when we were forced together. Alise was timid and barely made eye contact. I thought they were over-reacting. There hadn't been any other incidents. Secretly, I felt a little thrill at intimidating Zendra.

I was angry that Zendra had escaped the Mistress's judgment. What she had stolen from others was worth more than jewelry or scarves. She had stolen self-esteem. I hoped she had changed since I'd seen no bullying since Portia left. Maybe she was afraid of what would happen if she was caught. We were all more subdued.

I was relieved early in my second year when a letter from Sarah stated that Albair had not been chosen by the Masters upon turning fourteen. His mischievous nature would surely have landed him in trouble. I shuddered at the thought of him tied to a tree and screaming like Portia. Years ago, they would have blinded him, and before that, killed him. Perhaps being chosen was not such a blessing.

Two new fourteen-year-old girls came to the Sphere the second year, Prisilla, a short brown-haired girl with pink eyes, and Mandolie, a muscular girl with grape-colored eyes. Safia and I were asked to take them on the tour of the Sphere. We walked slowly, answered questions, and paused whenever the two girls wanted to examine something. Then Caari offered to take them on a tour of outside. When I tagged along, I realized Caari had discovered far more than I about the animals, forest and waters around the Sphere. My admiration for her rose.

Prisilla and Mandolie quickly became the best of friends and often socialized with Safia and I. Prisilla was a serious, studious girl whose insightful questions made me conscious of how little effort I had put into ethics class. She did not have the Vision of Tongues, instead her pink eyes held the Vision of Calm. Whether it was a distraught patient, a hysterical parent, an angry drunkard, or a frightened child, Prisilla would be able to soothe them. Her greatest ambition was to develop her skill well enough to become a mentor at the Sphere someday.

"I should like to become Mistress Pax," she said.

Mandolie, however, had the annoying habit of talking over other people whenever she wanted to speak. She also felt it necessary to dismiss other people's stories and tell a bigger one.

Safia took it in stride, but I would try to talk over her in return. I found the girl disrespectful. Shouldn't Mandolie be showing more deference to a second year girl? The Mistresses didn't even seem to notice her rudeness. I wished Portia was here to teach her a well-deserved lesson. Someone needed to. Otherwise, she'd probably turn into another Zendra.

XXIII

One evening we were lingering after supper, discussing our favorite home cooked meals. Safia had tried to speak three times, but Mandolie continually drowned her out. I felt my temper rising.

"The best meat pie I've ever eaten," said Hydie, "was one my father made for the Earl. I didn't eat that one, of course, I ate the practice one. It was stuffed with barley fed quail. The gravy—"

"That's nothing," interrupted Mandolie. She launched into a story about eating a swan pie at a duke's table that had gold flakes in the crust.

Was there ever a ruder phrase than "That's nothing"? I stared at her flap, flap, flapping lips. Did the girl never stop trying to be the center of every conversation? She made me feel as though nothing I said was worth listening to. Just like the snobbish girls in Wren River village. Why couldn't she just shut up?

Mandolie coughed dryly and reached for a water jug. Croaking and gasping, she filled her glass with water and downed it.

"Whew!" she said. "That was weird. My throat got so dry all of a sudden."

Safia looked at me; I feigned nonchalance. I turned to Hydie. "Tell us more about the quail pie your father made for the earl."

Afterwards, as we walked back to the common room, Safia leaned in toward me and whispered, "You did that, didn't you?"

"I don't know what you're talking about," I said as I pushed open the wooden door.

Safia followed. "You made her throat dry up. Come on, admit it." We walked over to our sewing boxes.

"All right, yeah, so what?" I snapped. "You don't know how many times I've wanted to and didn't. She infuriates me interrupting us all the time. She always has a better story. She actually raises her voice if I try to finish mine. She talks as much as the rest of us put together. She never passes up the opportunity to say how rich and connected her family is." We carried the supplies over to chairs by the large window, sat down on cushioned chairs with adjacent small tables and opened the boxes.

"I thought you swore off that kind of thing," said Safia as she searched for a needle. "We're supposed to use our Visions only for good."

"That was good." I unfolded my pieces of cloth. "I did it once out of about a hundred times when she deserved it. I think I should be congratulated for my self-control up to now."

Safia pressed her lips together and shook her head. "Maybe you should think about it during your self-awareness contemplations for the next while."

I coughed and looked away. "All right." Who had time for that? When I wasn't reading, I was practicing using my Vision. It was better to focus my energy on perfecting it and researching in the library. I had begun to skip contemplation periods again. I didn't have much faith in the techniques being taught. If the Mistresses were so smart, then why did they have to hurt nice girls like Portia and reward witches like Zendra? I had to admit, drying up Mandolie's throat was an act of defiance. I resented the control over our every move. Sometimes, I felt like a puppet. I wasn't going to hand over every scrap of independence because the Mistresses thought they always knew how everyone else should behave. In my heart, I was still Leya Truelong and I would make my own decisions.

128

We silently organized our work. Safia took a deep breath and said, "I'm not going home when we're finished our second year."

"Really?" I rested my sewing in my lap and looked at Safia. I was making a miniature Mistress's robe for a porcelain doll I had bought for Sarah.

"My family is already quite well off," said Safia. "Father is a skilled goldsmith. How's that for a coincidence? I am sure he would want to use me to become wealthier, and I would disappoint him. I know we would fight about how to exploit my Vision and probably wind up hating each other. Besides, I've stopped trying anyway."

She tied a knot and bit the dangling thread off. Even though Mistress Prophet and her assistants provided us with proper clothing, Safia enjoyed making her own and would often volunteer to help the Mistress. She enjoyed adding unique creative touches and was gaining a reputation as a skilled designer. Today she was working on travel-pants with closable pockets.

"Oh, that's too bad," I said. "My family has very little, but we don't fight. Not real fights, although my little brother, Albair, makes me crazy sometimes."

Safia unrolled a long blue thread and snapped it off. She licked the end and squinted as she threaded the needle. "Everyone in my family already fights about money, even though we have more than enough. However, my father is going to be furious that I have not fulfilled my potential. Either way, there will be nothing but trouble." She pulled the thread through the eye and knotted the ends together.

I resumed sewing. "My parents will want me to use my Vision to help as many people as possible. My Ma is always bringing food to the sick even though she is challenged to feed all of us. They will probably ask me to help others whether they can pay or not, which is fine with me, as long as I get to do some work for wealthy people and charge a whole lot of money."

129

Safia sighed. "I wish Mistress Sangra had never selected me."

I shook my head sadly. This was the best thing that had ever happened to me.

"For the two years of study," said Safia as she sewed, "the Sphere sends money to our families, to make up for our absence, and when you leave, you will send a portion of what you make back to the Sphere. I haven't made any money for anyone with my Vision, and I never will. I can imagine my father screaming about that. I just can't face it."

"What are you going to do?" I asked as I folded a tiny hem.

Safia set down her needle and stared into space. I sewed quietly, waiting for my friend to collect her thoughts.

"I've discovered that I have other skills," said Safia. "The Mistresses love my weaving and sewing. They asked if I would be the official seamstress. It seems Mistress Prophet is too ill to do much anymore. She's actually much older than she looks. I think I'm going to say yes. At least sewing doesn't hurt. I don't know how the rest of you can stand the pain in your eyes when you use the Vision."

I shrugged. Maybe farm work had toughened me. "I'm sure the Mistresses will be thrilled that you are going to be a seamstress," I said. "I know I was impressed when you told me you had woven and sewed your own clothes. I admired them the first day we met, especially your cloak."

Safia smiled. "Thank you. Silver, gold, they're basically just rocks that people covet. They have no genuine value. Now clothes, that's something we all need. Besides, I'll never lose a sewing needle for long. Just about the only skill I perfected is finding something metal nearby and for some reason, sewing needles are easiest."

"If I ever lose one in a haystack," I said, "I know who to call."

We laughed.

"Now finding water," said Safia, "that is priceless. I'd rather have a Vision like yours. Being able to find nickel deposits is not exactly life and death. I think the world will be fine without my potential being filled. But water. There's nothing more valuable."

I smiled. "Do you know what's happening with Caari? I hardly ever see her. She never eats in the hall, no matter the weather. I guess second year students can eat where they want. She doesn't talk during class, comes in at the last minute and is the first one out the door. You know, I've never figured out what her issue is with me."

Safia shrugged. "Caari's not returning to her village either."

"I've never heard her talk about her family," I said.

"I don't think she was happy there," said Safia. "She's not going to live in the Sphere either."

"Where then?"

"She wants a cottage in the woods, nearby. She said she'll continue to bring fish and game to the Mistresses and be available if they need her. I think she prefers the company of animals to people."

"Yes," I said, "she likes to be outdoors too."

"It must be hard for her to kill animals for food," said Safia.

"I never thought of that," I said. "She was dressed in animal skins when we first met her."

"Now she realizes she has an unfair advantage."

I thought how some people would like that. Caari had a higher sense of honor than I did. Is that why she was so aloof? I stitched, thinking about how complicated other people's lives seemed to be and how little I really knew the others.

"So," I said, "I guess I'm the only one from our group who wants to return home. I can't wait to see my little sister, Sarah. I've missed seeing her grow. I even miss my annoying brothers, Thomis, Maark, and Albair." I thought of their goofy grins and relentless teasing. I even missed the occasional punch in the shoulder. I didn't admit that, most of all, I wanted to see the look on Jenifair's face and the other wealthy village girls.

"I'm sure they'll be glad to have you home," said Safia.

I considered how much things must have changed in two years. "I think so, but after all this time, maybe they're used to not having me around. Maybe my sister won't want to share her bedroom again. Maybe my return will be nothing but a big disruption."

Clang! Clang! Clang! went the emergency bell. All Novices were to meet in the library at the sound of three recurring bells. We put down our needles and listened. The bell repeated, clang, clang, clang.

"What is it?" whispered Safia, her face pale.

"I don't know, but we have to hurry," I said as I dropped my sewing on top of the basket and took Safia's hand. "Whatever it is, it's urgent."

XXIV

Together we rushed through the hall toward the library. Mandolie and Prisilla were already there, as were Mistress Sangra and Mistress Prophet. Caari, the other Mistresses, and the hired help soon followed.

Mistress Prophet stepped away from the group and signaled for quiet. Safia still held my hand.

"May you always see clearly," said Mistress Prophet.

"May your vision be pure," we all responded.

"There is nothing to be frightened of," said Mistress Prophet. "We've called you here to make it easier for the Masters to search the premises."

"For what?" I said.

"It is actually a whom," said the Mistress. "We are not in any danger. However we wish to stay out of their way in order to make this proceed as quickly as possible. Two of the groundskeepers are helping with the search."

"Why are they searching for this person?" asked Caari.

Mistress Sangra and Mistress Prophet exchanged a glance. Mistress Sangra stepped forward.

"They are searching for a Renegade from the Master's Sphere of Vision. He has caused physical harm to another and has refused to stand trial."

"What harm?" I asked.

"The details are unimportant," said Mistress Sangra. "We must cooperate with our Vision brothers. They will not leave until they are allowed to do as they want." Her face was tight when she said this.

"Why do they think he's here?" asked Caari.

"That is enough questions," said the Mistress. "Take your contemplation position and expand your self-awareness on your responsibility to use your Vision peaceably." She waved toward the cushion. "Go now, everyone. Find a seat and start."

Wide-eyed Safia dropped my hand and went to get a cushion. I frowned and looked around. As everyone crowded around the cushions and sought a private spot, I saw Caari edge toward the exit. She'd better not go off on her own at a time like this.

Mistress Arbor touched Caari's arm and drew her back toward the cushions. Caari glanced around, frowned, and joined the group.

We sat for two hours. I felt as though caterpillars were crawling all over my skin. I wanted to know what was happening. Were the Masters searching our rooms? Why were they here? There was something we weren't being told. What had the Renegade done? Was it worse than what Portia had done? I didn't blame him for running. I would run too.

When the group was dismissed, both Caari and Mandolie quickly disappeared. Safia and I walked back to our sewing, speculating on the event.

At supper that evening, Caari joined us girls at the table. This was an odd day all around.

"Does anyone know if they caught the Renegade?" I asked.

"I don't think so," said Mandolie, "but they did find my stash of wine. The Masters wanted me punished until the Mistresses explained that I was simply practicing my Vision."

"Turning water into wine," said Safia. "I think you'll make a good living with that skill."

Mandolie shrugged. "Maybe, but it's not a big deal. And I don't really want to put legitimate wine makers out of business."

"You'll be a popular wedding guest, anyway," I said.

"Did you find out anything from your cousin about the Renegade?" Safia asked.

"Her cousin?" I said.

"Mandolie's cousin works in the stables," said Safia.

How did Safia always know these things about people?

"The Renegade burned his employer over some disagreement. When he was told to attend his examination by trial, he ran away. He was spotted getting on a ship for our island," said Mandolie.

I thought about the Sphere of Vision run by the Masters on the next island. Perhaps he was going to appeal to his mentor for help and had been forced to land here. No, that was impossible. The Masters were harsh. There would be no compassion shown there.

"Who was it?" asked Prisilla.

"Someone named Master Simon Wakefire," said Mandolie.

"Strange," said Safia. "What does he want?"

"No one knows," said Mandolie.

Caari stood up and strode from the room, leaving her food behind.

"What is with that girl?" said Prisilla.

"I wish I knew," said Safia.

"She's probably gone to search on her own," I said. "No one knows all the secret places on this island like Caari. If he's here, she'll find him."

"Oh, no," said Safia. "We'd better tell the Mistresses. No telling what he might do to her."

We rushed over to the Mistresses table.

"Yes?" said Mistress Sangra when we interrupted. We exchanged the correct greeting.

We explained our concern for Caari's wellbeing. Mistress Sangra nodded as she listened.

Then she smiled. "We thought she might. Someone is already following her to be sure she is safe."

I said, "How did you—"

"Go back to your table and finish your meal," said Mistress Prophet. "Everything is taken care of. There is no need to worry."

We gave a respectful bow and retreated. Mistress Prophet must have foreseen something.

"How weird was that?" said Safia.

"There is definitely something they aren't telling us," I said.

I was tired of the Mistress's secrets. The only way I would ever know what was going on and have a say in things, was to become one of them. I concentrated even more on perfecting my Vision and read everything I could about previous Mistresses.

I had a secret of my own. Having been told my green eye might signify another Vision, I researched the histories of Mistresses with green eyes. The most intriguing to me was the Vision of Growth. I thought I might as well start with that and work my way down to others if I failed.

Using what I had already learned about controlling the Vision of Water, I experimented with growth. Mistress Sangra had said it might be too difficult to master a second Vision, but I found the opposite to be true. The third day of practice, I was able to make a hibiscus bud open.

A month after my sixteenth birthday, Mistress Sangra came to my room and said, "You can return to Wren River now. I believe you will use your Vision well and be of benefit to all. Your abilities have surpassed my expectations. You are now a full Mistress of Water. You are entitled to wear the robes and choose your new last name."

I sat on the bed, chewing on my lip. Finally, I looked up at the puzzled expression of my mentor. "Thank you. I want to, but I feel I have more to learn. I have an itch for something more."

Mistress Sangra nodded, "I suspect you have the potential for a second Vision as well. One Vision can be enough responsibility and work though. Consider the demands on you, now and later."

I straightened my tunic and sat taller. "I want to try to master Growth," I said. "I've been practicing it on my own and I can already open flower buds. I read about other Mistresses with the Vision of Growth in the library."

"Clever girl!" said Mistress Sangra.

I got to my feet and smiled widely. "My combined Visions of Water and Growth could end droughts and famines." I studied

Mistress Sangra's face. "I want nothing more than to serve, to bring peace and happiness to others. I could help my village become a paradise."

"That's a good goal, if a bit ambitious," said my mentor as she raised her eyebrows.

I shrugged. "I need a supportive place to practice and there is nowhere better than here. Besides, there are books I still haven't read."

"Of course," said Mistress Sangra. "Stay as long as you require. Come to me whenever you feel the need, or any of the other Mistresses. However, I think you can work on your own. If you like, you can still attend classes. There is always more to learn."

I nodded. "I would like to choose Mistress Marina as my new name."

"A lovely choice," she said. "I will inform the other Mistresses. We will gather together when your gowns are ready to witness the taking of your second oath."

A few days later, there were two new white gowns and two silk robes on my bed, both shades of blue, with a note simply saying, "After the evening meal. Wear a robe." I ran my hands over the cloth. Not the finest silk, but still nice.

We gathered in the library. I loved the feeling of the gown against my bare legs. In the north, I would have to wear leggings underneath.

Mistress Sangra was beaming. All the Novice's and Mistresses sat on cushions, mixed together.

"Welcome my Vision Sisters," said Mistress Sangra. "We are gathered here to celebrate Leya's accomplishments and welcome her to the level of full Mistress."

I looked out at a sea of smiling faces. I had trouble believing the day had finally come.

Mistress Sangra and I stood together.

"Repeat after me," she said.

It seemed a lifetime ago since I had taken the entry oath. I had researched the final oath and was unsure whether I could say it. I meant to discuss it with my mentor, but didn't want to be pressured into compliance. Now the moment had come, and I still had no plan of action.

"I swear allegiance to the Spheres of Vision above that of family, community, country, and faith," said Mistress Sangra.

My heart leapt into my mouth. Ahead of family? Why would they expect that? I looked into Mistress Sangra's red eyes. What would happen if I didn't take the oath?

XXV

I took a deep breath. It would be my oath, my way, and whatever came of it would come of it.

I said, "I swear allegiance to the Spheres of Vision equal to that of family, community, country, and faith."

The silence rang in my ears. Mistress Sangra glanced out at the other Mistresses, unsure whether to continue. She looked back at me, cleared her throat, and continued.

"I will use my Vision to benefit others before myself, always with the needs of the Sphere in the forefront."

Might as well take the whole way. I said, "I will use my Vision to benefit others before myself, always considering the needs of the Sphere."

Mistress Sangra pressed her lips together, eyes blazing. She lowered the scroll.

The word Sphere seemed to vibrate through the library. Slowly, Mistress Denta got to her feet. She addressed the group, her slanted white eyes resting on each person in turn.

"We Mistresses have been negotiating with the Masters for quite some time to change the wording of the oath. I find Leya's version to my liking. I also believe an oath taken under duress is invalid."

Caari's face split with the biggest smile I had ever seen her give. She and Mistress Denta were both Miniria. I had wondered, at first, why Mistress Denta had not been her mentor instead of

Mistress Arbor, or the Caza people. But I realized they had both cared for her, in their own way.

I was the first of our group to take the oath. None of us had spoken of it but Caari must have felt as resentful as I did. Even though she seemed to have allegiance to no one outside the Sphere, she did not like to be dictated to or controlled in any way. I could see the other Novices were all smiling with relief, except for Safia, whose sweet face was scrunched in worry.

Mistress Prophet stood. "I have already taken the liberty of preparing Leya's version, should other Novice's wish to repeat it."

She pulled a scroll out from the folds of her gown. My mouth fell open. Mistress Prophet laughed.

"I told no one of my Vision," she said. "I wanted everyone to react according to their true feelings. I see that we are all nervous about breaking away from the Masters' direction. But I also see that we prefer Leya's wording."

Everyone nodded. There were a few murmurs of agreement.

"Excellent," said Mistress Prophet.

She stepped carefully through the seated Novices and Mistresses until she reached Mistress Sangra's side.

"All those Mistresses who would like to adopt the new version of the Second Oath, raise your hands."

One by one, hands went up, including Mistress Sangra. I wasn't sure if I could vote. Was I a Mistress if I hadn't said the official oath?

Mistress Sangra took the new oath from Mistress Denta's hands and nodded. She unrolled the scroll and read silently as Mistress Denta returned to her seat. Mistress Sangra looked at me over the scroll and said, "There are no more changes according to this. Are you content with the rest of the oath as it is?"

"Yes, Mistress Sangra," I said. "I am content, although I think the last part is pretty harsh."

"I agree," said Mistress Sangra. "Perhaps, once you are a Mistress, you can help us rewrite that part as well."

I smiled. I repeated the rest of the oath without pause.

"As long as I live, whenever I benefit personally from my Vision, I will send tribute to the Sphere of Vision. I will never take it upon myself to teach another how to use their Vision gift, unless it is under the direct supervision of the Sphere. I will risk all that I have and all that I am in defense of the Sphere and my Vision Sisters.

"If I break this oath, may my eyes crack and wither in their sockets, may all my sisters turn against me, may I be hunted like a rabid dog, and may I suffer the punishments of the damned."

Mistress Sangra took out a silver Sphere of Vision brooch. I would be able to afford a gold one someday, if I wanted, but I doubted it would mean as much to me as this one. I was surprised to see Mistress Sangra's fingers trembling as she fixed it to my robe.

"Mistress Marina, welcome to the Sisterhood of the Mistresses of Vision." She embraced me and whispered, "I always knew you would shake things up. I was never sure how."

A table of sweets and drink had been prepared. Mandolie turned our glasses of water into wine in celebration. "I'm learning how to make different bouquets," she said.

"Flowers?" I said, peering into my cup.

She laughed. "No, giving a different scent or taste to the wine according to people's preferences."

142

I took a careful sip. "Oranges!"

Now, I could sit with the other Mistresses at meals, if I wished, and not feel out of place. Instead, I usually wore my old clothes and sat with Safia.

I did, however, wear my new robes to the village the next time I attended the market. Shopkeepers bowed respectfully and many whispered as I passed.

At the Sphere of Vision though, nothing changed. I decided to learn as much as possible since there was no library in Wren River. I could afford to buy my own books, but the Sphere's library was vast and had one-of-a-kind selections, hand-written originals. Every Mistress wrote journals which were sent to the school at her death. These often held more information than the scholarly books.

Now that the pressure was off, I enjoyed the Sphere more. I especially liked biology. The better I could understand plants, the further I could control them.

I experimented with flowers, trees, grasses, vegetables, fruits and grains. At first the forced plants were altered in some way. The flower lost its scent. The fruit lost its flavor. I read more botany books, dissected the plants, and studied the inner workings of growing things. Gradually, my abilities improved.

Water and growth, there were no superior Visions. I had the greatest powers of all – those that gave life. Ma would be so proud of me.

Safia, also, attended classes, as well as Mandolie and Prisilla. There were no new fourteen-year-olds chosen that year. Now that I was a Mistress, I could ask any question, even the kind that wouldn't be answered in class.

I put on my robe and went to see Mistress Sangra.

"I'd like to know why no one was chosen this year? Did no fourteen-year-old girls show potential?"

Mistress Sangra rubbed her left temple, thinking. "There were three. We have added many more questions to the interview, and I was not satisfied with their answers."

"What do you mean?" I asked.

"Let's just say, stripping a girl of her powers is the most horrible thing a Mistress has to do. The Masters have insisted that we do not hesitate. If we do not do it, they may resort to blinding." She paused and gave a long sigh. "We need to be more particular about whom we choose. If you have to participate in stripping a young person's Vision, you will understand."

My whole body stiffened. "I'll never do that."

"You may have to, if you stay here and become a mentor."

"No," I said, "I'm going back to Wren River, as soon as possible. I want no part of that brutality."

The Mistress studied my face for a moment. Then she gave a soft nod. "It is brutal, but it is also necessary."

I headed for the door. I paused and turned to her. "Will Portia ever walk again?"

Mistress Sangra jerked with shock. I stared into her eyes, my chin high. She sighed. "She is under the best care we can provide, a former Novice of mine. She is walking, slowly but with more control. She is also starting to speak."

I nodded and left. Speak! I hadn't considered that she might have lost the ability to communicate. Social, funny Portia, trapped inside her head. I felt sick to my stomach.

I never put the robe on again while I was at the Sphere, not even for shopping. I did not want to be included in their decisions.

144

I wanted to be left alone. I pushed myself all the harder so that I could leave sooner.

In botany class, I asked numerous questions. I was trying to understand how to determine when climbing ferns crossed the line from attractive to nuisance.

"They're so lovely," said Mandolie. "How could anyone ever consider them a pest?"

"When they crowd out other plants," I said.

"Just move the other plants somewhere else," said Mandolie.

I wondered if there was a minimum intelligence test Novices had to meet before they were selected. Perhaps that should be added to the interview.

I took a deep breath and said, "Some of those other plants are trees. Not so easy to move."

"Well just plant more then," said Mandolie as she shrugged her muscular shoulders. "I think you're wasting your time reading stuff like that."

I felt my temper rising. How could this girl be so stupid? Why didn't our teacher ever tell her to shut up? Mandolie was wasting our time with ridiculous comments. I could make her shut up. I did it before.

I looked into Mandolie's purple-blue eyes. She smiled back. I felt my power thread through my body, aching for release. Just a dry throat. That's harmless. Then I glanced at Safia. Her silver eyes studied me, waiting to see what I would do. Fine, then. I'd let Mandolie rattle on and on. It wasn't my fault if no one could get a word in. With a scowl, I buried my face in my book.

When class ended, Safia walked with me to the dining hall. We chatted about the lesson and what we might have for lunch.

I wondered if Safia knew how close I had come to losing my temper. She never seemed to lose hers. She had self control before she even came to the Sphere. I wondered what she got out of all those hours of contemplation. I couldn't remember when last I could spare the time for sitting and contemplating. I didn't need to squander precious hours on self-examination. All I had to do is remember my moral boundaries and stick to them. Easy as blueberry pie.

XXVI

Over the next year, the Sphere of Vision had record harvests thanks to my help. My Vision of Growth became as developed as my Vision of Water. The flowers bloomed longer, the fruit was sweeter, and the grains were tall and golden. People at the market greeted me by name and some hired me to heal sick trees, encourage growth in the fields, or purify their wells. I knew I was held in high regard.

At age seventeen, I was ready to return to Wren River village as full Mistress of Growth and Water. I had read everything of value in the Sphere library and learned as much as I could from the teachers.

Every five years a Vision Recorder would come to my village to collect tribute and to learn how I had been using my gift. Random people would be interviewed to ensure I had not broken my oath.

Since Sarah and I still exchanged monthly letters, my family was aware of my progress. They must have bragged about me to other villagers. I received a letter from the mayor pleading for me to return to the community that loved me. My friends, especially his daughter Jenifair, had missed me. I laughed so much, I started to choke.

However, I felt as though I needed a big dose of reality, and my brothers would be sure to provide it. All this bowing and thanking was giving me a swelled head. And, more than anything, I missed my family that loved me and accepted me just as I was. I purchased two horses, one to ride and one to carry the numerous bags of clothing, jewelry, and gifts.

Safia's face puckered when I went to her room to say goodbye. "I never had a sister," she sniffled. "You're the closest. You've been more than a Vision Sister to me."

I hugged her. "There'll be new Novices, and they'll be glad you're here."

"I can't teach them anything," said Safia.

"Nonsense. You can teach them to sew, to work hard, and to be a good friend. You're the best example of what the Sphere of Vision should represent. They're lucky you're staying."

"I don't think I can bear to walk you to the boat," said Safia, her eyes swimming with tears.

"Just as well," I said with a sad smile. "I don't want to cry in front of the sailors and start some kind of storm that will sink the ship before I even get on it."

We both laughed. This was almost as difficult as leaving Sarah behind.

Mistress Sangra met me by the exit. "You've come a long way, Mistress Marina," she said. "I was a little worried about you at the start. Your mother worried too, I suspect. I think that's why she wanted me to keep an eye on you."

"Thank you, Mistress Sangra. For everything. You made it so much easier to be away from home."

Mistress Sangra kissed me on both cheeks and then looked into my eyes. I remembered the first time I had trembled under that gaze. This time, I stared directly back and smiled.

Caari was waiting for me in the stable. I was surprised. I hadn't thought Caari would come to say goodbye. I wished I had gotten to know her better.

"Your horses are ready," said Caari. "They're good mounts, though this one"– she patted the brown pack horse – "likes to eat too much for her own good."

"Thank you Mistress Wild. You didn't have to do that," I said.

There was a stable-master who would have fed, watered, and saddled the animals.

"Just wanted to be sure you would be all right." Caari helped me tie my bags to the brown horse's saddle. We turned awkwardly to each other. "Take care of yourself, Leya."

"You too, Caari." I placed my hand on her shoulder. "Please visit Safia often. I think she might be lonely."

Caari nodded and then passed me the reins of both horses. I led them down the path toward the dock. I turned once to wave goodbye, but Caari was not in sight.

The crossing was invigorating, but far too short. I was the only Mistress on board. This time, I controlled my emotions as I watched the orcas frolic in the frothy waves. I felt a surge of loss when I disembarked. I hoped that wouldn't be the last time I sailed on the ocean.

From the Mistress who taught geography, I carried a detailed map marked with all the best inns along the way. I was a little nervous riding alone, but soon realized my robes were more protection than the thickest armor. Only once did I receive a disrespectful look from a surly-looking man. He had very bad teeth and a jagged scar that ran through his left eyebrow, eyelid, and cheek. At first, I thought he was licking beer from his lips, but then I realized it was a suggestive movement aimed at me. I went to the innkeeper and told him to deliver the food to my room.

I did not rent the largest rooms, but chose comfortable and modest accommodation. Still, it was better than anything my parents had ever had.

The eighteenth night I had difficulty falling asleep. The terrain was more familiar, some similar plants and trees to those around Wren River. I felt homesick and anxious for the trip to end.

I knew I could summon the innkeeper for a mug of warm milk, but decided instead to go downstairs. There were half a dozen men lost in their cups as I sat at a corner table. One, with very bad teeth and a jagged scar, stared at me, his mug tightly wrapped in his two hands. I flinched when I recognized him from the previous inn.

I waved for the innkeeper. He put down his dish towel and came to my table.

"If there is anything the Mistress would like, I can bring it to your room," he said, bowing and showing his bald spot.

"I need a change of scenery," I said. "Just a mug of warm milk, if you have it. My name is Mistress Marina."

"Of course, Mistress Marina," he said. "That will take a little time."

"Good, I feel a need to walk. I'll be back soon." I would not be treated like a prisoner nor would I live like a child afraid to venture outdoor on my own. I was a Mistress of the Sphere of Vision and I would not be mocked.

"It's dark outside," said the innkeeper.

"I'll be fine," I stood and smoothed my clothes.

The innkeeper shook his head, lips pressed together, but said nothing more.

As I stepped out the inn door, darkness closed around me. Overhead, white stars poked holes in the black felt sky, and the moon hung like half an orange. I followed the path toward the stable, my fine leather boots beating a rhythm on the hard-packed earth. I turned right, sensing a stream somewhere out of sight.

150

Trees and bushes closed in around me, pulling at my silken robe. I focused and they pulled away, clearing my path.

It was a small stream, and none too clean. My nose twitched at the smell of sewage and gutted fish. Anger rose from my belly. How could people treat water like this? Such disrespect. Didn't they realize that without clean water, everything dies?

A large figure came crashing through the trail behind me. I turned. In the feeble moonlight, I recognized the scarred customer from the inn. I knew from his leers he was up to no good.

XXVII

"I warn you to leave now, while you can," I said.

He laughed drunkenly. "Not until I have your purse," he said. "And some fun with that fine young body."

"Fool," I said. "I am a Mistress of the Sphere of Vision. You would do well to keep your foul hands to yourself."

"Not likely," he said taking a step toward me.

I concentrated. A creeper twined itself around his ankle, causing him to crash to the ground.

"Hey!" he shouted. He cursed me, threatening to do even greater harm.

I summoned the grasses and plants. My eyes burned with pain but that only made me angrier and more determined. The vegetation threaded over his body, climbing his grimy clothes, wrapping around his face, gagging his mouth. His shouts became mumbles and then whimpers. Covered in growth, he was barely identifiable as human.

Shaking with anger, I wished I could send the plants up his nose and down his throat. He would be dead in minutes. The plants would soon digest his body. No one would ever know.

"Vile idiot," I said. "I assume this path is used by the people who live close by. I smell their filth in the water. One will come down this path tomorrow, or the next day. If you haven't been eaten by wild animals by then, they can cut you free. Until then, think on how you will treat women in the future."

As I walked past him, the trees reared back to let me through. He struggled and grunted in vain. The trees closed behind me. I couldn't suppress a giggle at his complete helplessness.

By the time I had reached the inn, my temper had cooled. I decided to tell the owner. If the drunk was eaten by a wolf or bear, I would be held responsible. Or what if the plants smothered him? His thrashing about might cause his own death. I would be charged with murder. Damn. I hadn't thought this through.

"Innkeeper," I called. "I need your help."

I related what had happened on my walk. The innkeeper apologized for the confrontation and sent two men to free my prisoner and escort him to the local sheriff. I was requested to write a report on the incident which would be used to determine his punishment.

In the morning, the other guests stared at me and whispered among themselves. It was a different feeling than when the villagers on Vision Island watched me in awe. There, they had whispered in admiration and excitement. Here, it seemed they monitored my movements with distrust and even fear. It reminded me of the way Zendra had reacted. I left as quickly as I could.

I arrived in Wren River at midday. Two farmers bowed in respect, stopping in their work to watch me ride by. I wondered if they recognized me. With my splendid clothes and horses, I could be any Mistress from a distance. Even though I was the same size as when I had left, I sat taller and with more confidence.

Our home looked well tended, as did the yard. I hesitated at the door, wondering if I should knock. I pressed my ear against the door, listening carefully. When I was sure I knew where everyone was in the room, I flung open the door with a crash, laughing as I did so.

My sister, clearing dishes from the table, dropped a wooden bowl in shock. My father and brothers froze as they were just about to leave the table. Ma, eyes wide, stared and then gasped and rushed forward to hug me tightly. Then she stood aside, studying me from top to bottom.

Sarah, now ten years old, almost eleven, had grown in height. She stood beside Ma, hesitantly smiling at me. Sarah's clothes were simple, but clean and whole, much better than when I had seen her last. I was suddenly conscious of my own silken robes trimmed with silver. I must have seemed like a stranger.

"I don't even get a hug from my little sister," I said. I pushed my bottom lip out in an exaggerated pout.

Sarah laughed, stepped forward, and threw her arms around me.

"Well," I said, "not so little anymore." We hugged and rocked, as my brothers thumped my back and messed my hair. I felt wonderful.

"Trouble's back in town," said Maark.

"Don't expect us to call you Mistress," said Thomis.

I laughed. Nothing like family to keep you real.

Sarah pulled back and ran her hands over my blue and green robe. "This is so soft, like butterfly wings."

I smiled, "You always did have a touch of the poet."

"You look like a princess," said my sister.

"Are you willing to let me share a room with you again?" I asked.

"No need," said my father. "The Sphere of Vision sent enough coin for building supplies. I've added a large room on the back just for you."

"They didn't tell me it was so much," I said.

"They said you earned it," said Ma.

Sarah tugged at my skirt. "So?" she said.

"So? What?" I asked.

Sarah put her fists on her hips and pouted. "Where's my present?"

I burst into laughter. "Now, that's the little sister I know and love. It's in my bag. Only, I didn't realize how much you had grown. You might not like it."

I carefully removed the bundles around the doll until there was just one cloth and passed it to Sarah. Sarah's eyes widened as she peeled back the linen to reveal the doll dressed in a Mistress's red robe, a tribute to my mentor.

"It's beautiful!" she squealed, "Just like you."

I sighed with relief. "She has a travelling outfit and other clothes as well." I looked around at my smiling family. "There are presents for everyone."

I gave a warm sable cape to Ma who ran her hands through the luxurious fur. "This is too extravagant," she whispered.

"It will keep you warm on the coldest days," I said.

Ma nodded and rubbed the fur on her face. "Thank you, Leya."

"Pa, I brought you some new tools. I hope you haven't already replaced your old ones. I remember you said you wished you had a better set of chisels. I hope these do the trick." I passed my father a small chest.

He looked up at me, wonder in his expression. Slowly, he unclasped the latch, lifted the lid, and looked inside. "My word," he said, "flat and gouges. Thank you, daughter."

I gave Albair a compass and a set of maps to study; he planned on traveling when he was older. For Maark, there was a short knife with an elaborate silver handle and a thick leather sheath with his name embossed on it. Thomis, the family accountant, received a set of pens, one silver, one ivory, and one mahogany and a book of crisp white paper.

To my family, these were all wondrous treasures. But to me, they were just the beginning.

XXVIII

Over the next months, I transformed our farm into a paradise. The pain of using my Vision of Growth lessened. No one grew sweeter fruit, larger vegetables, or heavier grain. We harvested more than we could eat or preserve. The excess sold at market for prime prices.

My family's standing had already risen in the community, thanks to the coin they'd been sent, but now, having a full power, Double Visioned Mistress as a daughter made them the most important people in the village. Matrons pushed their sons in my direction; I was the most eligible woman in the district. Other villages sent proposals as well. I was embarrassed by the flood of mail, many with tokens and gifts, and the constant stream of possible suitors.

One letter made me blush.

Dear Mistress Marina,

I hope soon to call you Leya, as I have learned that is your personal name. It is a very personal relationship that I wish to forge with you. I too have a Double Vision. Together, we would be unstoppable. The world could be ours to share through a long and happy life. I understand you are a young woman, which pleases me. I believe you will find me appealing. We could sire magnificent children.

How repulsive. A man I had never even met proposing to breed with me as though I were a mare for sale. I stopped reading and tore up the letter. I asked my parents to screen any future proposals and let me know if they felt there was anyone I should see personally. All this attention would surely corrupt me. I had no desire to turn into Jenifair.

"Though, I'm in no hurry to become betrothed," I said.

"Good," said Ma. "You're much too young to marry yet. Besides, I'm a believer in letting love take its course. Your father and I found each other, and when the time is right, you will find your perfect match as well."

"I don't see that happening soon," I said.

As usual, Ma was right. Months later, it was Ballard, a miller, who changed my mind. I had not really noticed him before I left, at least not in that way. I had been a girl of fourteen and him a grown man of eighteen. Now the difference in ages no longer seemed awkward.

Several times I spotted him picking up grain and delivering flour. My pulse quickened as I watched him lift the heavy bags. His bright hair flashed in the sun and sweat gleamed on his muscular arms.

I thought of him as I walked through our fields, imagining him by my side. I thought of how his hand would feel in mine. I wondered if he would be intimidated by a Double Vision Mistress. But, whenever I saw him, it was me who was intimidated.

Each time I encountered Ballard, it seemed more difficult to walk without stumbling. I found myself staring and forced myself to look away. Then I was concerned he would think I was snubbing him, so I tried to smile, but my lips formed an awkward grimace. It was impossible to speak. I knew my voice would be shrill and nervous. Around him, I did not feel like a confident, powerful Mistress. I felt like a foal taking its first steps.

As I walked by the stream one morning, I spotted him unloading bags of grain from his wagon outside the mill. He had removed his shirt, revealing sculpted and gleaming abdominal muscles. My legs felt weak; a thread of desire bubbled in my belly like a hot spring. I swallowed twice, unable to speak a suitable greeting.

"Greetings, Mistress Miraculous," he said, with a bow, as I neared.

I laughed; it sounded high and silly to my ears. "Mistress Marina," I said.

"Ah, a much nicer name, though the villagers call you Miraculous, I shall not."

"You're Ballard, right?" I asked, as though I hadn't whispered his name to myself a hundred times.

"Yes, I am. You may not think so, but you and I, Mistress Marina, have a lot in common." He leaned back, setting an elbow on the bags in the wagon.

I glanced at his rippled abdomen. The triangle of dark hair on his chest was damp with sweat. A drop was poised above his belly button. I stared, fascinated. Water, the Vision of life, never looked so desirable. I fought the urge to touch it.

"Don't we?" he asked.

I blinked, "Pardon?"

"Have a lot in common?" He grinned.

I looked into his ruggedly handsome face, and shrugged, trying to appear nonchalant. "I don't know what you mean."

Ballard waved his hand toward the grain and stream. "You're Mistress of Water and Growth. I'm master of water wheel and grind. We both improve on what nature provides."

"Oh, I guess that's right," I said.

"So, did you use your Vision of Growth on yourself?" he said.

I lifted my arms outward from my sides. "I'm still as short as ever."

"True, but you've grown up in all the right places."

I giggled. I should have been offended, but a tingle ran through me, all the way to my toes. He had noticed me as much as I had noticed him, and he liked what he saw.

He winked and hoisted another bag. I was mesmerized by his clenching muscles, confident smile, and casual attitude. I was Mistress of Water and Growth, wealthy, powerful, and even revered. How could this simple man make me feel like a nervous baby chick?

It became a daily habit, to walk by the mill and chat with Ballard. Often, we simply discussed the crops and the weather. I did not point out that I could control both, but expressed the same concern over rainfall and sunshine as anyone else. Then our conversations turned to other issues, the decisions of the town council, our families, our interests, and our hopes for the future.

One day, we had a long conversation on the raising of children.

"I'm glad we see eye to eye on so many things," said Ballard. "Good day to you, Mistress Marina."

"Please, call me Leya," I said.

He smiled. "Thank you, Leya. 'Tis a beautiful name for a beautiful woman."

As I watched him carry the bag into the mill, I realized I might be Mistress of two Visions, but he was master of my heart.

The first time he kissed me, it felt as though thousands of butterflies had burst from my body and swirled around us. Although his hands were strong and calloused, when he touched me they felt as silken as river water over my skin. Under his touch,

I did not feel like a Mistress or a village girl, I felt like a part of him, a part of the earth, the sky, the water, a part of every living, beautiful thing in existence. The desire for power seemed ignoble. Fine clothes seemed trivial. All I wanted was to look into his eyes and see love, see his breath quicken, and feel his lips on mine. Spending the rest of my life with Ballard was the sweetest vision of all.

XXIX

Our wedding was set for my nineteenth spring. Ballard built a four room cottage adjacent to the mill. Together we whitewashed the walls.

"I guess I will never have to want for fruit and vegetables," said Ballard.

"Nor flax, nuts, or lumber," I said. I grinned. "How do I know you aren't marrying me for my eyes?"

"How do I know you aren't marrying me for my muscles?" teased Ballard.

"Oh, you conceited man!" I said.

"I saw you watching me unload the bags of grain," Ballard said, a sparkle in his eyes.

I blushed. "I guess we both have special gifts."

Ballard paused to drink from the bucket of water, and then passed the dipper. "Should we have four daughters and six sons, or five of each?" he asked.

I sputtered, spilling the water down my work clothes.

Ballard grinned. "You are Mistress of Growth."

"We'll see," I replied, laughing as I wiped my face. "There can be too much of a good thing."

Safia made the wedding gown. She visited Wren River to take my measurements.

"Well, Mistress of Growth, you've certainly grown," she teased as she measured my bust. She jotted down the number in her tiny notebook.

"Too much of my Ma's good cooking," I admitted. "I think Ballard likes me round rather than the stick girl I used to be."

"I have a few gown ideas that will make his eyes pop out of his head when he sees you walk down the aisle," said Safia.

I grinned. "Show me, show me."

Safia took out her sketch book and spread it on the table. "I was thinking the gown should be a blend of blue, green and gold, for obvious reasons."

"Blended like the cloak you were wearing when we first met?" I asked. "I loved the way the fabric shimmered."

Safia tapped her chin with a pencil as she thought. "No, much better than that. This one is going to seem as though it moves, like water."

"Oh, I like that." I squeezed Safia's arm. "You're magic with cloth. That's your real Vision."

We poured over the sketches long into the evening. Safia spent several days with me, even though she could have afforded good accommodations in town. We caught up on news about each other and the Sphere of Vision. She had stopped on the way to visit Portia, who was now well enough to speak in sentences and walk with a cane. Mistress Sangra and Mistress Denta were visiting her frequently for healing sessions. Knowing she was improving was the best wedding gift of all.

I enjoyed having a room to myself since I had returned, but it was also nice to have company again. My family loved Safia. We parted with hugs and laughter.

Three moons later, the dress arrived.

Sarah gasped as I held it up. "Is it enchanted?" she asked.

"Just the enchantment of a talented weaver and seamstress," I replied as I held it in front of my body and looked into the mirror. "Safia has her own magic."

"I love it. Everyone will," said Sarah as she carefully traced the waves of color with her fingers.

"I hope one person in particular does," I said. I laid it out on the bed. "Go get Ma. I want her to see it when I try it on. I hope it fits."

The morning of the wedding, I pinned white Miller's Blossoms in my hair. It was a small affair, immediate family and friends. I wanted intimacy, not a lot of gawkers and socially ambitious villagers trying to increase their status by pretending to be my friend. Jenifair brought me an early gift, hoping for an invitation, but I thanked her and left it at that.

Safia helped me prepare, tucking and shaping the dress in all the right places.

"It fits perfectly," I said with a twirl.

"I'm more proud of this than anything I've ever made," she said, "and you're the perfect person to wear it."

Ma stood by, occasionally wiping her eyes, while Sarah danced around as though she had hot coals in her shoes.

My attendant, Widow Freya, by tradition the eldest village woman, stayed with me while the others left for the hall. She helped me step into my new white satin shoes.

"Almost time," she said.

I wished Safia or my mother could have remained with me until the ceremony instead of this dry, old stick of a woman. Freya still wore calve-length black dresses, a striking contrast to her long white hair. Surely she could have worn something more cheerful for my wedding. She had been a widow in mourning for as long as I could remember.

However, I knew my family and friends were waiting for me in the hall with my future husband. They would be smiling and cheerful and dressed in all the colors of nature. They would get to see what Ballard was wearing before I did.

I wondered how he would look. He would not tell me what he was going to wear. I had never seen him in anything formal. I knew I would be as delighted as he when our eyes met. In this dress, I would be unforgettable. Would he—

"Fire! Fire!" My thoughts were shattered by the cry.

I clutched the skirt of my gown and ran through the door and down the street, Freya trailing behind.

A crowd reached the hall and organized a bucket brigade shouting to be heard above the roar of the fire. Flames shot through the thatched roof of the old wooden building. The farrier dipped his cloak in a bucket of water, wrapped it around his bulk, and tried to enter, but the vicious heat drove him back. Others threw ineffectual buckets of water. The huge timbers groaned as the fire rampaged.

Inside, were Pa, Ma, Sarah, Thomis, Maark, Albair, Safia, Ballard and his family, and our closest friends. It wasn't possible. It was a nightmare. I forced myself to stop screaming and stilled my mind. I had the power; I could save them. I focused on the sky, envisioning dark clouds rolling in.

As the rain sprinkled on the roaring flames, the hall roof collapsed with a thunderous crash. How had it spread so fast? I clenched my fists, filling my mind with rolling, thundering cumulonimbus clouds. They formed overhead, swirling angrily. Tears streamed down my face. Rain hammered the earth. Muddy water swirled over my white satin slippers.

"Mistress Marina, it's too late," said the farrier as he gently touched my arm.

I flinched. No, it couldn't be. How could this happen? My powers were useless against death. I screamed, tearing at my wedding gown, ripping the skirt to shreds. What use was it now? Ballard would never see it.

I fell to my knees as the fire cooled. Blackened, cobbled beams hissed. Wisps of steam and smoke twisted upward like writhing dark spirits. No one inside had made it out.

Finally, Widow Freya touched my shoulder. "Come, child," she said.

I was taken back to my family home, now empty of loved ones.

For weeks, the village was deluged. I couldn't stop crying. Waves of sorrow, anger, and frustration rolled over me like a tidal wave. I wanted to stop, but I even woke up in the middle of the night, crying. Too much rain ruined the crops. Muck was everywhere. Mudslides tore the hills apart. The river swelled and overflowed its banks.

I knew I had to leave before my grief destroyed the village completely.

XXX

I traveled slowly on my way back to the Sphere. The journey helped me gain control of my emotions. Everywhere I had looked in Wren River, I saw reminders of Ballard. Here, I was free of memories of him.

Mistress Sangra welcomed me back. After I told her of Safia's death, and all my loved ones, she embraced me. As she rubbed my back, she whispered, "Caring for others is the best method to find your way out of the pain."

I nodded. I felt numb, emptied, like a dry well.

Mistress Sangra sent childless villagers to me for treatment. The challenge of using my Vision in a new way was a distraction. I pressed my hands against their bodies, coaxing fertility where there was none before. I massaged stunted children, stimulating their bones and muscles to stretch and grow. Daily I thought of Ballard and those who had died, but every time I helped to ease the suffering of others, mine became a little more bearable.

I sought out the company of Caari. Caari, however, was seldom in her cottage and almost never came to the Sphere of Vision. We were always happy when we did see each other, but it was too seldom for my liking.

Mistress Sangra, and my other former teachers, became familiar company, but I was unable to form the same kind of friendship with anyone that I had had with Safia.

But, I was loneliest of all for male company. In my short time with Ballard, I realized I was happiest as part of a couple. Would I ever have the opportunity to feel that way again?

Two years after my return, Mistress Sangra brought me to an inner chamber of the Sphere. Elder Mistress Prophet lay in her bed, face pale, eyes clutched tightly in pain. Mistress Denta sat in a chair by the bed. She carefully dabbed a little water onto Prophet's lips with a white cloth.

"How can I help?" I asked.

"You can't, my dear," said Mistress Sangra. "She is dying."

"I am Mistress of Growth and you can heal her blood. We can send for Babetta and Minuetta, perhaps the four of us —"

"It is her time."

"I pressed my fingers to my lips.

Prophet opened her eyes and nodded weakly.

"As you know, Mistress Prophet carries The Power of The Veil," said Mistress Sangra.

"Yes."I knew that it protected the carrier from fire, water, and weapon. I also remembered it was passed to another when the bearer was dying. The Veil worked for the Mistresses only. The Masters had not yet found one among their own kind. I glanced at Mistress Denta who nodded. What did I have to do with any of this?

"Step closer to the bed," said Mistress Sangra.

Trembling, I approached the dying woman. Mistress Prophet took my hand in her claw-like one. Her green eyes flew open and stared into mine. Her grip tightened; I flinched as my knuckles ground together. How could an old, dying woman have such strength? Mistress Prophet's body lurched, became rigid, and her eyes rolled back in her head. She shook violently. I whimpered.

"Do not let go of her hand," commanded Mistress Sangra.

Mistress Prophet's eyes returned to normal. She stared into my face. "Listen carefully," she croaked. "You are the one, but it is not for you."

"What—"

"Sha!" said Mistress Sangra.

Mistress Prophet continued. "I give you The Power of The Veil, but you will not have it for long. You are the carrier. When you come in contact with the true host, it will surge from your body and enter hers."

She paused, exhausted. Mistress Denta helped her take a drink.

"You must protect it until then," whispered Mistress Prophet. "Are you chaste?"

"Chaste? Oh. Yes."

"You must remain so until The Veil leaves your body. Can you do that?"

"Of course," I said. Part of me could not imagine being with a man, other than Ballard, and he was gone. Forever. Part of me knew that, someday, I would be ready. But where would I ever find someone like him?

Mistress Prophet closed her eyes and let out a long sigh. A soft light shimmered from her body, rising upward. It floated toward me and wrapped around me. My skin tingled and my eyes stung. Mistress Prophet dropped my hand. I swayed, light headed. I hadn't agreed to anything, but it was too late to protest now. Besides, it would only be for a short while.

Mistress Sangra took my shoulders and led me to my room.

"Rest for a while," said Mistress Sangra as she sat me down on my bed.

"What does this mean?" I asked.

"It means that while you carry this gift, you are protected. No arrow, knife, fire, lightening, water, fist or foot can harm you when you cast The Veil."

"Wow."

"However," said Mistress Sangra. "Should you lose your virginity, the Power of The Veil will become dormant, unusable until it is passed on to your successor. She will then be invincible."

"Why did Mistress Prophet choose me?" I asked.

"She did not," said Mistress Sangra. "The Veil chooses."

"How did you know to bring me to her then?"

"I have brought many Mistresses in to see her and the three Novices. Do not be insulted, but you were not my first choice."

My face warmed. I thought I had proven I could control my impulses and bank my temper.

Mistress Sangra touched my shoulder. "Frankly, since you have two Visions, I did not think it would be you. You already have immense power. Besides, I know how you feel about stripping another of the Vision. The carrier of The Veil is sometimes called when none other can subdue a Renegade."

"I see."

Mistress Sangra smiled and patted my shoulder. "Lie down for a while and rest. It is a shock to your body, I am sure. It is only temporary. The recipient will probably be one of the next fourteen-year-olds who come to the Sphere."

I sighed as I settled back, waiting for the light-headedness to pass. I wish they had given me more time to think about it. I really didn't want this "gift". What if I met a man who could fill the hole in my heart left by Ballard's death? How long would he wait for me?

As I poured the purified water into the brass jugs, reflected torchlight twisted on the surface. Droplets fell into the pink coral reservoir creating concentric circles. An open building had been constructed over the spot where the spring water surfaced, but water birds often nested underneath and fouled the water. I saved the Sphere of Vision hours of straining and boiling the drinking water.

"Leave the containers," said Mistress Sangra as she entered. "The village of Hawthorn has asked for our help and I believe you are the best suited for this task."

"Can't I finish this before I meet them?" I asked.

"They are not here," said the Mistress. "You will have to go to them. I will send someone else to carry the jugs."

"Why can't they come here?" I asked as I tucked a strand of hair behind my ear.

"You have to go to their village to solve this problem," said Mistress Sangra. "It is in the Caza region. Besides, you have not left the Sphere since your return two years ago. It is time you re-entered the world."

I scowled and wiped my damp hands on my robe. "Caari has not returned to the world. She still lives alone in that little cottage in the woods."

Mistress Sangra shook her head. "I do not think Caari was ever part of the world. She admits she was always separate from others, more at home with animals than people." She turned and gestured for me to walk with her. "I suspect there are things about her life that we can only guess at. And you, my dear, are not Caari.

The world needs you in it. You are a social woman at heart. Besides, our Visions are for everyone." We walked down the coral pathway and into the Sphere proper.

I opened and held the door for my mentor. "The last time I tried to return to the world," I said, "it didn't go very well, for many people, including Safia. She planned on staying here, and if she had not left to come to my wedding, she would be safe today."

"You do not know that for sure," said Mistress Sangra as we walked down the hallway.

"I know she wouldn't have died the way she did. What's to say calamity won't strike me again?"

"I cannot guarantee anything," said Mistress Sangra. "Life is filled with twists and turns, many unpleasant. However, this time you have The Power of The Veil to keep you safe and those close to you. There is no one better equipped for this task. You cannot hide here forever."

"There are others who have never left the Sphere," I said. "You didn't."

Mistress Sangra nodded as she stopped in front of a large supply cupboard. "I am not you and at least I travel for the selection once a year." She opened the large mahogany door and pulled out a travel bag. "It will be good for you to get away. You may even decide to stay, which I would be glad to see." She shut the door and continued walking toward the bedrooms.

"Stay in Hawthorn?" My brows puckered.

The Mistress shrugged. "It was once a lovely village, but it has suffered greatly. You can renew it."

I opened my bedroom door. "How? What's wrong?"

Mistress Sangra entered and placed the travel bag on the bed. "The worst drought in their history. Nothing grows. The villagers are starving."

"I see," I said. "Of course, I'll go."

"Good," said the Mistress. "You leave tomorrow after breakfast."

After she left, I flopped down on the bed beside the bag. The thought of entering a village, perhaps like Wren River, made my stomach tighten. How many young couples would be watching me? How many families would expect me to save them? How many little girls would be waiting for the great Mistress Marina to fix everything? I didn't know how I could face it.

How could she even suggest I stay there? I would be surrounded by young men all too eager to marry a Mistress of Vision. Perhaps there would even be one who could love me for myself. How would I explain that our relationship could never be consummated as long as I carried The Veil? But then, perhaps I would find the next recipient and be free of this burden. Mistress Sangra had not said it had to be someone with the gift of Vision.

XXXI

It was the protective power of The Veil which gave me the freedom to risk crossing the Wildersands. Still, the thought of travelling through a barren, infamous desert took some of the joy out of the upcoming ocean crossing.

The next day, Mistress Sangra ate breakfast with me. "I sent a servant to load your bag and prepare your horse," she said.

"Thank you," I chewed thoughtfully on the rye bread.

Mistress Sangra continued. "Oafling is at the dock with his donkey. He is a simple man, but honest and dependable. You will be safe with him."

I followed my mentor along the worn coral stairs, breathing deeply, trying to stem my anxiety. I had not left these cloistered walls for two years, yet the pain suddenly burned like yesterday. I was a very different person from the impulsive fourteen-year-old who had gaped with delight at every new sight. I wondered if my mother would be proud of the quiet control I now demonstrated.

Oafling's droopy eyes widened when I approached leading my great black mare, my green and blue cloak with gold trim snapping in the wind. He nodded. I smiled as he struggled with his kicking and braying donkey, trying to get him on to the catamaran.

Under the grime, wild black hair, floppy grey hat and tattered bulk, Oafling was respectful and competent. He spoke broken Esfera with a heavy Cazalese accent. The ocean did not appeal to him the way it did to me. He spent the entire journey below deck and refused to surface until we put into port.

The first morning at an inn, I found Oafling asleep outside my doorway.

"What are you doing?" I asked.

He lumbered to his feet, tidying his clothes. "Keeping Mistress safe."

I chuckled. "I am as safe as the sun. You do not need to worry. If I pay for a bed for you, I expect you to sleep in it."

"Yes Mistress," he bowed his head.

As we travelled, I rented rooms for the both of us and paid for our breakfasts and suppers to be brought to our rooms. I no longer risked eating in the common room since the incident with the scarred man.

I remembered my first journey with Mistress Sangra, Caari, and Safia. I hadn't spoken to Caari much since my return to the Sphere except for occasional exchanges when Caari helped with the animals or brought fish to the kitchen. I did feel, however, that she had finally warmed to me.

We rode for six days, staying at inns along the way. Oafling seldom spoke, and I found the rhythm of riding contemplative.

The seventh day we reached the Wildersands. Trees gave way to turpentine bush, prickly pears, and brittle bush.

"Are you sure you want to cross here?" I asked.

"Mistress Sangra say you not come to harm in desert," he replied.

I grinned. "It's not me I'm worried about."

"I tough," he sat up tall in the saddle, his jaw set firmly. "My dark skin good in sun. You too pale. You burn."

"I'll be careful." I nudged my mare forward.

Oafling made camp each evening and built a small hot fire from charcoal nuggets he carried. Making fire was a challenge for me whose Vision of Water hampered this simple skill. Oafling killed small animals like lizards and ground squirrels and harvested edible cactus. These he cooked on the coals.

As Oafling poured my tea, I asked, "Why were you chosen to petition?"

"Ma spoke at town meeting. Said Oafling deserves chance. Chieftain say no loss if I not return."

I frowned. "I'm sure it would be a loss to your Ma and your friends."

Oafling tilted his head. "Ma cried. Lent me lucky comb Father gave her." From his breeches he pulled an amber comb.

"It's beautiful."

Oafling smiled and passed it to me. I admired the delicately carved roses entwined around the name "Marissa." I passed it back. "Is Marissa your Ma?"

"Yes," Oafling nodded. "Works hard. Pa died. Hard life with no husband."

I flinched.

"I make you sad," he whispered. "Stupid me."

"No, not you." I sighed and looked off into the deepening twilight. "The comb reminded me of someone I lost."

Oafling slipped the comb back into his pocket. "Share sadness with friends, not so sad."

176

I looked into his large, serious face. "I should like to be your friend, Oafling."

"Yes!" he smiled. "Have many friends. Widow Bowen bakes me cakes; I plough. Help Tom Gentry forge; he clip my donkey's hooves."

"You're a hard worker," I said.

"Not all work." Oafling smiled and gestured widely. "Many children friends. They ride on my back. We laugh. Children small, but important."

I passed my hand across my forehead.

Oafling's brow furrowed. "Sad still."

"It's alright," I whispered.

"We rest," said Oafling lumbering to his feet. "Tomorrow reach worst Wildersands." He gathered up the pan and dishes. "Few plants. Few animals. No water. You make rain if we run out of water."

"If there's water, I can find it," I said as I watched him rub the pot, plates, and forks with sand. "I can draw it up from the ground. Making it rain where it never rains is not a good idea. It isn't wise to interfere with ecosystems."

"Not wise to die either," said Oafling solemnly as he wet a cloth and gave the dishes a quick wipe.

As we travelled, grass gave way to dry sand. The trees disappeared, exchanged for tumbleweeds and cactus. My horse stumbled occasionally in the deep sand; it was slow going.

We travelled early mornings and evenings. The copper-colored desert was stark and silent. Fragments of baggage and bones broke the monotony of sand, the remnants of unlucky travelers. Dust crept into our hair and clothing. Our eyes ached from the dry glare. Grit irritated our teeth. The inside of our noses cracked and stung.

"Sandstorm!" shouted Oafling as a wall of darkness approached. He jumped off his donkey and pulled me off my mare.

"We must get under cloaks," he shouted. "Little chance we survive. Sorry. Horse and donkey no chance."

"Trust me," I said as I pushed his hands away. "We will all survive."

For a second I wished I'd mastered Air instead of Growth and Water, I could just blow the sand in a different direction, but Mistress Prophet's legacy would protect us. Mistress Sangra had explained how it was used. I prayed my first attempt would be successful.

I rotated slowly and then raised my arms to fling The Veil sealing me, Oafling and the animals in safety. The air crackled and sparked; the sound of the wind became muted. Sand battered the shield that had formed around and above us. My horse reared; the donkey brayed and kicked.

"Must wrap animal's eyes," said Oafling. "They hurt us or themselves in fear."

I remembered the way the sailors had blindfolded the horses so they would not panic on the small catamaran. Together, we subdued the frightened animals, dodging kicks. I wished Caari was with us. She could easily control the terrified mounts.

The storm lasted the better part of a day. Inside our bubble of safety, we sipped water and consumed cooked rabbit from the day before. Oafling watched the sand strike the barrier, a million tiny impacts, and slide to the ground.

"Is powerful magic Mistress has," he whispered.

When the storm ended, sand was piled twice as high as our heads on the windward side.

"Come over here. Get as close to the side of the bubble as possible," I said as I led the animals away from the overhang of sand. "I'm worried that when I collapse The Veil, the sand will fall and bury us."

Oafling grimaced, eyes wide, and stood beside me. I whirled slowly. The cliff of sand trickled, and then folded down in a sudden rush, burying the rabbit bones where we had sat.

"Wow," said Oafling. "Glad we moved."

An hour after we resumed our travel, Oafling halted abruptly. "Look!" He pointed.

"What is it?" I asked.

"Is horse."

"Horse? Out here? Why would a horse—" I gasped in realization at the pile of sand.

XXXII

We quickly dismounted. I held both sets of reins while Oafling dug. Beside the dead horse was a buried man. Oafling stepped back, frightened. I stepped forward, passed the reins to Oafling, knelt, and gently peeled a cloak off the victim's face.

The man's hair was dark and curly. His skin was dark, his face long and lean with high cheekbones and a pointy chin. Caza. He was older than me and wore an eye-patch. He was so still, prickles rose on my skin. An image of Ballard, buried in ashes, flashed through my mind. I pressed my fingers against his throat, searching for a pulse.

"He's alive. Oafling, get the water bag. I think he's from your region. Do you know him?"

Oafling brought the water, stared at the man's face, and shook his head no. I dripped water onto the victim's lips and trickled a bit into his mouth. He moaned and opened his grey eye.

"Drink," I said.

He swallowed three large gulps and then whispered, "Thank you."

"I am Mistress Marina and this is Oafling," I said.

"Simon Freeman," he whispered.

We helped him sit up and clean the sand from his clothing. He coughed, blew his nose several times, and then took a long drink.

"I am in deep gratitude, Mistress Marina," he said.

180

Once recovered, Simon Freeman joined us. We loaded his saddlebag on the donkey. Together Simon and I rode the mare. I was conscious of his strong chest pressing against my back. I could feel his wiry body flexing against me when he moved. Sweat trickled down my spine like exploring fingers.

"Why did you take such a risk?" I asked. "Crossing the Wildersands, alone?"

"I received word my father died. My Ma needs me as I am her only living child. I thought the stories of the Wildersands were exaggerated. I took the quickest route home."

I felt his shrug, a nonchalant masculine movement.

I sighed. "Quickest is often shortest, but not in a good way. Your Ma almost had two griefs."

"You're right, Mistress... What is your birth name?"

"Leya Truelong." It slipped out before I had thought to protect my privacy and distance.

"Mistress Leya. Lovely." His breath was a hot breeze caressing my neck. "It was foolish. I should never have taken such a risk. But then, if I hadn't, I wouldn't have met you."

I knew I should tell him to call me by my honorific name, but Leya sounded melodious when he said it. It had been so long since I had heard my name on a man's lips. Not since my wedding day.

Time winged past. Simon Freeman was an entertaining and charming companion. He told stories of his travels and I was reminded of how little of the world I had really seen. His misadventures and odd encounters made my cheeks ache from laughing. It had been too long since I felt so good in the company of another.

He asked many questions about the Mistresses of Vision Island.

"I've never seen anyone with two different colored eyes," he said. "Are there many Mistresses like you?"

"None that I've met," I said.

"The Mistresses sound much nicer than the Masters," he said.

"How do you know?" I asked.

"Just rumor," he said.

After several days, we entered a less severe part of the desert. The twisted trunks of cottonwood signaled the presence of water. I asked the men to stop and slid from my horse. Using my Vision, I called it to the surface so we could fill our depleted water bags.

"That's some trick," said Simon. "Travelers will be grateful for this new oasis."

"No," I said. "I will return the water to its natural course."

Simon scrunched his face in puzzlement. "Why? It could save someone else's life."

I tilted my head and said, "At a cost of everything that depends upon the underground stream. All life is sacred."

Simon frowned, but said nothing. "The way of those with Visions is strange to me."

Pipe cactus and white gravel ghost flowers broke the monotony of sand as we travelled. Soon desert willow and mimosa